DON'T KISS ME

FARRAR, STRAUS AND GIROUX NEW YORK

Farrar, Straus and Giroux
18 West 18th Street, New York 10011

Printed in the United States of America
First edition, 2013

Some of the stories in Don't Kiss Me *originally appeared in the following publications: "After" in* Dark Sky Magazine, *"Birthday Luncheon" in* Red Lightbulbs, *"Brenda's Kid" in* Wigleaf, *"CANDLES" in* PANK Magazine, *"Clocks" in* Burrow Press Review, *"Dallas" in* trnsfr, *"Dishes" in* Knee-Jerk, *"DON'T KISS ME" in Orange Alert's* Hair Lit: Volume One *anthology, "Gerald's Wife" in* Sundog Lit, *"A Girl" in Fifty-Two Stories'* Forty Stories *anthology, "Heart" in* Burrow Press Review*'s "15 Views of Orlando" series, "Like" in* Paper Darts, *"Me and Gin" in* Barrelhouse, *"My Boyfriend Del" in* Annalemma Magazine, *"Nixon in Retirement" in Melville House's "Forty-Four Stories about Our Forty-Four Presidents" series, "Our Man" in* MAKE, *"Plans" in* The Handshake, *"RV People" in* BULL {Men's Fiction}, *"Splits" in* Midwestern Gothic, *"Summer Massacre" in* Denver Quarterly, *"Three Things You Should Know About Peggy Paula" in* Fifty-Two Stories, *and "You and Your Cats" in* Unstuck.

Library of Congress Cataloging-in-Publication Data
Hunter, Lindsay, 1980–
[Short stories. Selections]
Don't kiss me / Lindsay Hunter. — First edition.
p. cm
ISBN 978-0-374-53385-4
I. Title. II. Title: Do not kiss me.

PS3608.U5943 D66 2013
813'.6—dc23

2012049024

Designed by Abby Kagan

www.fsgbooks.com
www.twitter.com/fsgbooks • www.facebook.com/fsgbooks

1 3 5 7 9 10 8 6 4 2

for Chicago

CONTENTS

DON'T KISS ME

THREE THINGS YOU SHOULD KNOW ABOUT PEGGY PAULA

One. In high school Peggy Paula worked as a waitress at the Perkins. Night shifts were her favorite, kids from her school would come in after games or dances with bleary eyes and messy hair and Peggy Paula knew they'd been drinking and smoking those flimsy joints she'd see them passing, the girls with smudged makeup and rat's nests in the back of their heads, proud unblinking eyes, scanning the dining room like I dare you, I dare you to guess what I just let Jared or Steve or Casey do to me, I let him and I liked it and I don't care, and Peggy Paula felt honored just to be near these girls, envious, taking their orders for French fries and ranch, keeping their secrets and the sticky lipgloss tubes they'd sometimes leave behind, watermelon and cherry and berry and once a spicy cinnamon that burned Peggy Paula's lips for an hour, what kind of girl wanted burning lips, poison lips, Peggy Paula's heart pounding at the thought of such a girl, of the boy who went after such a girl in the backseat of his father's sedan, the girl stinging his lips, his neck, moving farther down, burning that boy up with her mouth, Peggy Paula going into the bathroom stall and wanting to touch herself but not knowing where to begin, wanting to begin everywhere, standing with her fists clenched and breathing hard, and then needing to be out from the stall and moving and so going back to the dining room feeling every inch of her skin, her lips cherry red and raw when she saw her reflection in the toaster, and three weeks later asking the redheaded dishwasher to drive her home and directing him to the spot she knew those girls went to, her lips aflame when he pulled up, sliding over, the stick shift digging into her hip, putting her mouth on his freckled neck, it smelled like mashed potatoes and industrial soap and sweat, her hand first on his thigh and then crab-crawling to his zipper, it was already hardening under there despite him saying, Hey hey, what, and Peggy Paula saying, Just, please, and the dishwasher quiet after that, letting Peggy Paula, letting her, following her into the backseat, holding her tight when it happened, saying, I'm sorry, and Peggy Paula saying, Shh, stinging his shoulder with her lips and his back with her nails and feeling filled up and afraid and like her heart could kick the windows out.

•••

Two. Peggy Paula has a kidney-shaped scar on her lower back from falling out an open window backward at a disco. She was there to meet men, but all the men at this disco seemed more interested in each other, though she couldn't be sure. She found a place by a window so she could see the men coming and going, moving her feet side to side, the disco just a warehouse with walls of windows and colored lights with roving beams, a purple lightbeam getting her right in the eyes and Peggy Paula holding her clutch up to her eyes and backing away from it and right out the window, the music so loud and the lights so frantic that nobody noticed. She fell into the Dumpster, staring up at the dark starless sky, her head nestling perfectly in the butt part of an old baby seat once it became clear she wouldn't be getting out on her own any time soon. The DJ cycled through "Jive Talkin'" twice before she was finally found, Peggy Paula not being able to help singing along despite her numb toes, despite the smell of rotten apples and wet cardboard and pee. How is there pee in the Dumpster, it seems real inconvenient, Peggy Paula was thinking, and I swear seconds later, she'd say, seconds later a boy in a sequin robe thing stood on some milk crates so he could pee into the Dumpster, his blond head looking up, and Peggy Paula still singing to herself so instead of screaming Hey or Stop she screamed TRAGEDY, and the boy so startled that his pee shot out and piddled the empty TV box just to the left of Peggy Paula, and he couldn't stop, him apologizing, Oh God sorry, Oh my God lady, I'm so sorry, my idiot dick I can't stop, I can't stop, and Peggy Paula just waiting it out with her eyes closed, thinking how it smelled like warmed butter, or buttered popcorn, something comforting like that, thinking it was kind of nice, kind of intimate, and suddenly feeling grateful for the whole night—the torturous application of blue eye-shadow, then green, then back to blue; the realization that her new dance move made her armfat shudder like tapioca in the pot; the eye contact she made with a mustachioed man who squinted, getting her into focus, then turned away; the crippling barbed loneliness that drove her out into the night and all the way to this disco—it was all worth it because it boiled down to this lovely private moment with a polite blond boy, who drove her to the hospital so she could get fourteen stitches and an ankle brace, and on the drive home told Peggy Paula she had a pretty face, offered her a small white pill to take that made Peggy Paula long to be naked, and the blond boy came in and lay on the couch with Peggy Paula watching late-night television, moved closer and stroked her jaw, her nape, pet her arms, her thighs, even gently pulling her knees apart and moving the back of his hand softly, lovingly, between her legs, Peggy Paula thinking, I am his pet, thank God I'm his pet, Why are my clothes still on? and falling asleep during a rerun of *Andy Griffith*, waking up to find the blond boy gone and her wallet and breath mints missing from her purse and a note that said, Thank you I'm sorry Thank you You're special. Peggy Paula loves that kidney-shaped scar.

Three. Peggy Paula was returning a video when she met a man she would love. He took the video from her like it was delicate and valuable, touching her wrist with his thumb and smiling. The man had a dimple in his chin and a wedding ring, that thumb on her wrist like she was his and he was making it known, and Peggy Paula had him over for pot roast and ice cream two nights later and lowered herself onto him so slowly that he cried out in frustration, Peggy Paula still stunned at this man before her, wondering how exactly it had happened, and then when he grabbed her hips to move her the way he wanted not wondering about anything at all. It went on this way for months, the man coming for dinner and Peggy Paula bathing and perfuming herself all day and wanting to pound the walls into dust with the waiting for him, telling him over and over how much she loved him, her mouth in his neck and her voice weak, like it had been diluted, the man grunting approval and Peggy Paula breathing breathing breathing breathing him in, the sour smell of video cleaner and his aftershave and underneath it all the smell of his wife's rosewater perfume, the same Peggy Paula used, and one day the man didn't come, and he didn't come the next day, and the next day his wife came and Peggy Paula remained calm, invited her in, and the woman also seemed calm, going into the kitchen, and Peggy Paula wondering if she felt comfortable enough to get herself something to sip, and the woman coming out with Peggy Paula's bread knife held high in her fist and making a horrible sound with her mouth, then Peggy Paula realized the woman was sobbing with her mouth wide open, and her heart broke for the woman even as she lunged, Peggy Paula wanting to show the woman how a bread knife doesn't have a point, is only good for sawing things, not stabbing really, but instead she moved out of the way and the woman tripped on the carpeting and stumbled toward the couch, the sobbing noise getting louder, and then the man rushed in and batted the knife out of his wife's hands, picked her up and carried her out of there, his eyes cutting over to Peggy Paula like it was her with the knife, her with the animal noises that wouldn't stop, and Peggy Paula so stunned that she couldn't cry, couldn't feel, and maybe that's why she let the man in two nights later, had to see his eyes, had to feel again, and she kept letting the man in, she kept letting the man, his smell the hair on his chest the delicate skin above his pelvis the muscles in his thighs his calloused hands the shapes of his toes the gold in his eyes the missing molar the mole on his back the heart in his chest the breaths in and out he was alive he was another he was a man and Peggy Paula let him, she let him, because if no one is there to touch you are you even really there?

AFTER

After the apocalypse, which stopped being a shock to the system after you saw them mallwalkers being vaporized over by the P.F. Chang's that you used to eat at with your momma at every birthday, idiots pumping they elbows like the sun wasn't an oozing boil, one of them a hawk-faced sculpture of bone before the rapture, so the pile of ash was an improvement, and why you was so angry at these ladies you didn't quite know, but it just seemed retarded, caring about your physical fitness while nearby four crows picked at a halved lady's crotch, but anyway after you crawled out the basement and your momma made you eat canned for every meal, after your brother's eye just one day burbled and dripped out the socket in yolky clumps that he wiped off with his shirt hem, after you found yourself prizing your goobers like the pig to the truffle, the moist dark ones you imagine having the most nutrients, after your daddy stopped wearing pants and you stopped feeling alarmed at his swinging wrinkled scrotum, after you watched your daddy's pimpled buttcheeks rumble with fart while he was staring dumbfounded out the window, formulating a plan he said, after your daddy took off besocked but bare-assed on your brother's bicycle, your momma making like to run after him but then shrugging and scratching herself, which is what she started to do after it was clear there wasn't no help coming, no tanks no army man no superhero no angel no wizard no god no God, your momma took to scratching herself, your brother took to rubbing himself through his gym shorts, both of them in a daze, these were comforts, after you saw the neighbor lady wave to you from the roof and then throw herself off, the body snapping when the rope caught and then blam, it crashed through her front room window, after your momma had you and your brother cut her down and your momma said, She always kept them flowers tidy and your brother said, She had sweet titties for an old lady, after your brother filleted the neighbor lady and you roasted her upper arms over a trash fire and salted them with dirt and had a regular chow down and then the next night you ate her inner thighs, which to you tasted like buttered rubber, after your brother tied one of the neighbor lady's breasts over his no-eye till it was greened and shriveled, after a priest came to the house asking could we smother him, or punch him in the throat till he was dead, or he don't know, stomp his head into a pudding, he couldn't do it himself, after your momma sent him down the road to the Circle K where that could be arranged, after you thought about having relations with that priest before he died because you never had and you couldn't with your brother, what with that eye, after you nearly said it, but then your daddy's privates flashed across your brain, that arid peachfuzz desert of a nutsack, that shriveled defeated wiener, and you let the priest walk on, after you watched your brother's baseball coach come down the road and stop to take a bite out his own arm, screaming and chewing, after your brother said, He always was a fuckin pussy, your brother rubbing himself, them gym shorts no bigger than a pair of undies now, all shredded and shitted cause your brother just went wherever he was, and why not, once you nearly ate a plump turd that toppled out his shorts into the dirt cause it looked just enough like a juicy sausage link, and cause you knew it'd be nice and hot, after you woke up and saw a baldheaded lady riding your brother's bicycle, your daddy riding the handlebars, you knew it was him cause his ass was out, after you didn't tell no one cause what was the point, after your brother lodged an old marble he found in the neighbor's yard in his empty eye socket, after he complained it itched his brain, said he was like to dig your momma's eye out and use it for his own, cause she don't do nothin with it anyway, old curdled cow, he always was embarrassed by your momma's cellulite problems, which persisted unchecked despite there wasn't no junk food to gnaw on, after you told him that wasn't respectful, after you had a dream a mouth with a burger tongue and onion teeth was eating you, after a woman in a ashy pink suit came to the door trying to sell a tin of blusher, after your brother said he'd give her a nickel for it, after you saw your brother and the woman humping against the side of the garage, your momma not ten yards away in a lawn chair, ash fluttering down on it all like the opposite of snow, after you asked after the blusher and your brother said, Oh yeah but didn't hand it over, after a fire came and you saw a pack of dogs outrun it, after your momma decided to live in the shower, after your brother started eating gravel, swallowing each pebble like a difficult but necessary pill, after your brother malleted the rest of the roof off cause he was bored, after you agreed boredom was the worst, far beyond the hunger and the fear and the fat chewed-up gumwad that your ear had become, after you woke to your brother curled up around a tattered stuffed elephant you didn't know he had, after he muttered, Eat your boob meat in his sleep, after you heard it before you saw it, after you thought maybe your brother wasn't asleep, maybe it was a lit fart, after that second white sting, after that clap of light, after

MY BOYFRIEND DEL

You got a eye booger, Del tells me. I can't look at it, it's sick. You all gooey. A goober goo-face. This he finds funny, he laughs loud, his mouth huge, all teeth but for where a ridged half-tooth is working its way down in the front. I try but can't get a purchase on why it was so funny, but even so I laugh too, I work out the eye booger with my fingertip and try to be demure when I wipe it on his momma's carpet. All the magazines say it's important to laugh together, laughter is important in any successful relationship, I laugh until Del gets distracted by his Transformer and tells me in his Transformer voice that it's time for me to die. I die over and over, wilting into the carpet, one time I wilt onto his laser gun and he tells me to quit being a stupid dummy. This hurts, I pretend I have to use the bathroom, I run the water and cry a little.

When I get back Del asks me, Number one or number two? but I don't answer, I never know how to answer that.

Later we drive to the Arby's for milk shakes. That's something any other woman might get agitated about, having to always be the one who drives, the one who pays, but I like that about me and Del. He's content just being taken.

You remember when we met? I ask him. He's playing with the radio, a preacher shouting a woman moaning an old hillbilly crooning the news the weather the traffic. Yeah, he says, you was in the library same as me. He goes rigid, then a machine-gun fart rat-a-tats out from him and he relaxes. Scuse me, he says.

That's right, I say, we both like books about aliens. Isn't that something?

This tastes like barf, Del says, but he keeps drinking. We are quiet for a while, which is a relief cause it can be difficult, getting a nine-year-old to conversate. I drive around the parking lot, into the next parking lot, maybe we'll go into the store and look at Legos, sometimes we do that, sometimes Del lets me take him to the ladies' clothes area so I can get his opinion on tops.

This is boring, Del says, and I get scared he's talking about us, so I rev the engine and pretend like I'm going to ram into an old woman with a shopping cart. Yeah, Del screams, I want to see her guts!

Back at his house he asks if I want to play Princess Leia and I am touched, I know he'd rather have her for a girlfriend than me, It'd be an honor, I tell him, and he hands me my lightsaber and then knocks it out of my hand with his. You're dead cinnamon-bun dumb-hair, he says, looking up at me through his bangs, my hand is throbbing from where his lightsaber hit, again I die for him, I shudder and quake and cry out and fall at his feet and die. Now I'm going to maybe spit in your hair, you don't know, keep your fat eyes closed, he says. Okay, I whisper.

Dinner, Del's momma calls, and I stay dead, waiting for Del to ask if I can stay and eat, but when I open my eyes a moment later he says, You gotta go.

I get up on my knees and hold my arms out, Del lets me hold him, he smells like sweat and his momma's shampoo, Herbal Essences, the pink kind, I checked. I squeeze him extra long cause I can't get up the nerve to kiss his cheek, maybe next time. I'll miss you, I say. Let go, he says, you acting like a butthole uglyface.

I pass his momma on the way out, standing at the stove in her housedress. You know I don't like you coming around so much, she isn't looking at me, just watching her own hand move the spoon around the pot. You a nice lady but my son is nine years old and you are what? You are what? I want to say I love your boy Del but I never even said that to Del yet, so I just leave it be.

On the way home I stop and buy a can of Beefaroni, me and Del can eat the same dinner even if we ain't in the same place. Over the program I watch I can hear Del's momma saying, You are what? You are what?

Del has a new friend, this Simon child with glasses and a neon snotlip, he is over every afternoon now, the first time we meet I offer him a tissue and he tells me I should use it to wipe the old off my face. We drive to the Arby's and Del sits in the backseat with Simon, I watch Del's face in the rearview, I wait for him to look at me but he doesn't, when we get to the Arby's I tell them I don't have no money even though I have fourteen dollars in a roll in my purse. On you? I ask Del, I am turned around and with a jovial look on my face, this is a adventure, my face is saying. Del says, Huh? and Simon says, We ain't got a dime, lady, we ain't even double digits yet. On you? I ask again. Let's just wander the store, Del says, and my middle flutters cause I love when he is decisive. Hold my hand in the parking lot, I say to Del, for safety. In the magazines they talk about how important touch is, affection, showing instead of just telling. In high school I held a boy's hand at a football game, the boy's hand rigid and cold in mine, the lights exploding around us and the air smelling like pizza and hot dogs and bubble gum, the boy got up to use the restroom and took his cup of 7UP with him and did not return. Go on, I say to Del, holding out my hand. Not a chance in heck, he says, he has recently learned to belch, the word heck comes out in a moist growl.

In the store Del and Simon race to the drinking fountains, Simon gets a mouthful and gleeks it at my slacks, says, Oh hey, pisspants, Del points and laughs. In the magazines they say men are sometimes cruel because they are testing your emotional boundaries, I want Del to know I am boundless, I am a universe, I grit out a smile and follow them to the toys, they arm themselves with swords and commence to stabbing me, Simon saying, Lop off her tiddies, Simon saying, I wish these blades were real, and I wish you were dying like old ladies are supposed to, Del chops me in half. A woman smiles at me, says, Boys, I want to tell her Del is my man, tell her he is not a boy, but she is wearing a pink hair clip and a wooden necklace and this convinces me she would not understand. In the video games aisle I stand behind Del as he and Simon shoot at homeless people and prostitutes, I wait while they throw basketballs at each other's crotch, I buy them hot dogs and Simon says, I knew you was lying about the money. I wait outside the bathroom while they relieve themselves, Simon comes out and says Del barfed up his hot dog, I don't know if this is true or not. In the recreation area Simon and Del spin the wheels of the hanging bikes and dare each other to stick their fingers in the spokes, I am desperate for Del to look at me, for his gray eyes to meet mine, all I require is a single moment, it is all I need in this world, I cannot go home to the bed and the walls and the single channel on the television and the white plate on the table and the drying tulip from Del's momma's garden without my moment, and I know what the magazines say about jealousy being a powerful motivator when a man can't commit, I grab for Simon and push my lips onto his, his smell like mold and ketchup and dirt, his heart beating out his whole body, his lips cold and wet, the snot, the snot, I pull away and he is wiping his mouth and gagging, the snot smeared across his cheek now, a glistening wing, his glasses fogged, Simon saying, What? What? Del emitting a high whining *ewwwww*, all eyes fixed on me, marbles of horror, I back away, I turn and walk through the blender aisle the baby clothes all the lotions and powders and mints and magazines asking me questions about myself, me thinking, How should I know? Me wondering why they don't say nothing about a kiss being salty as a tear.

CANDLES

I AM IN THE CANDLE SHOPPE I CAN'T HELP IT

THE NEW AUTUMN LINE IS ORANGE NUTMEG AND IT IS AS CLOSE TO BARF AS THE BOTTOM OF A DIP CUP

I DIPPED ONCE RIDING IN THE CAB OF THE TRUCK OF MY ONE TRUE LOVE, HE WAS DRIVING HE WAS GETTING A HAND JOB FROM A PUERTO RICAN PUTA WE WERE GOING ABOUT FIFTEEN MILES AN HOUR NOT EVEN ENOUGH FOR THE WIND TO LIFT MY HAIR IN A POWERFUL FUCK YOU WAY

I HAD STOLEN THE DIP AND THE CUP AND NO ONE NOTICED

THERE WAS A WEB OF JIZZ ON THAT BITCH'S SKORT, I SAW IT WHEN WE STOPPED FOR CIGARETTES SHE STOOD IN THE MAGAZINES AISLE DOING NOTHING

THAT WAS A LONG TIME AGO

JULIAN IS THE MANAGER OF THE CANDLE SHOPPE HIS ASS IS LIKE TWO HALVES OF A BASKETBALL I HAVE TRIED MANY TIMES TO TOUCH IT

MY FAVORITE SCENT IS BEACH SANDALS, IT IS SALTY

MY SON CALLS IT BITCH SANDALS

MY SON IS FOURTEEN HE IS ALWAYS STANDING WITH A BOOK A TOWEL A HAT HIS FOLDED CLAMMY HANDS COVERING HIS CROTCH HE DOES NOT KNOW I KNOW AND IT IS BETTER THAT WAY

I READ THAT IN A PARENTING MAGAZINE

WHEN JULIAN DESCRIBES SOMETHING AS "EARTHY" I KNOW WHAT HE MEANS IS "SHITTY"

I HAVE NEVER KNOWN A MAN WHO HAS MORE THAN TWO SYLLABLES IN HIS NAME

I HAD A DREAM JULIAN WAS SHOWING ME A CANDLE THAT WAS CALLED SUCK IT LIKE A STRAW

ITS COMPANION SCENT WAS LICK YOU LIKE AN ICE CREAM CONE

I HAVE NEVER BEEN ATTRACTED TO A MAN OF A DIFFERENT CULTURE BUT THAT ASS I AM NOT MADE OF STONE

I AM FONDLING A CANDLE SET CALLED HERBACEOUS TWILIGHT, I WANT TO ASK JULIAN WHY IT'S NOT JUST CALLED OLD FORGOTTEN BONG BUT HE IS HELPING AN OLD MAN OBSESSED WITH THE SMELL OF LAUNDRY

I HAVE FOUND THAT THE CANDLES WITH THE PRETTIEST COLORS ARE ALWAYS THE FOULEST, I WOULD LIKE TO HAVE SOME GREEN CANDLES BUT THEY ARE ALL CUCUMBER MELON

CUCUMBER MELON SMELLS LIKE AFTERBIRTH

I BREATHE WITH MY MOUTH OPEN WHEN I'M IN THE CANDLE STORE

SOMETIMES I AM SITTING AT HOME WITH A CRAVING AND I CAN'T PUT MY FINGER ON IT AND THEN BLAMMO, I WILL REALIZE I AM CRAVING THE TASTE OF THE CANDLE STORE

IT HAS A TASTE, I'M NOT ON GLUE

I JUMPED THAT PUTA BEHIND THE P.E. TRAILER, SHE PULLED MY HAIR AND SCREAMED AND I PUNCHED A TOOTH INTO HER THROAT

I TRY NOT TO FEEL VICTORY THINKING OF THAT

IT IS DIFFICULT NOT TO

I GOT INTO THAT BOY'S TRUCK AND TOLD HIM WHERE TO DRIVE AND WHEN HE PULLED OVER I CLIMBED INTO HIS LAP, THE LOOK IN HIS EYES

I LOVE THINKING OF THAT LOOK

JULIAN IS ASSURING THE MAN THAT THE FRESH COTTON CANDLE SET SMELLS EXACTLY LIKE BOUNCE DRYER SHEETS ONCE LIT

I KNOW THIS IS NOT TRUE, I KNOW IT ACTUALLY SMELLS LIKE KOOL-AID BACKWASH

THE OLD MAN IS ASIAN, I CAN SEE THAT NOW, THERE DIDN'T USE TO BE BUT ONE ASIAN IN THIS COMMUNITY BACK IN THE DAY, THE HIGH SCHOOL ALGEBRA TEACHER, BUT NOW THEY ARE EVERYWHERE, I SMILE EXTRA BIG AT HIM TO LET HIM KNOW I AM COMFORTABLE WITH OUR MULTICULTURAL SOCIETY

AND I AM

COMFORTABLE WITH IT, I MEAN

THE OLD MAN IS TELLING JULIAN HE HAS THE ORANGE NUTMEG LINE IN HIS DOWNSTAIRS BATHROOM, I FEEL SYMPATHY FOR THE SWIRLING VOMITOUS TOMB HIS HOUSE MUST BE

THERE CAME A DAY WHEN I RAN OUT OF CLASS TO BARF UP AGAINST THE LOCKERS, THERE WAS A BABY FOR A WHILE BUT THEN IT WENT AWAY

THE LORD TAKETH, THANK GOD

THE TRUCK BABY IS HOW I CAME TO THINK OF IT

I NEVER TOLD THE BOY, BUT I WISHED I HAD TOLD HIM SO HE COULD THANK ME FOR NOT TELLING HIM

JULIAN HAS FINISHED WITH THE MAN, I SEE HIM FIDDLING WITH SOME PAPERS AT THE REGISTER, I KNOW HE IS HOPING I WILL LEAVE

I WANT TO TELL JULIAN THE BESTSELLING CHILDHOOD SUMMER CANDLE HE SOLD ME LAST WEEK SMELLS LIKE BUBBLE GUM WEDGED BETWEEN TWO FUNGUS TOES

SOMETIMES YOU KNOW WHEN YOU SHOULDN'T SAY SOMETHING

IF JULIAN WERE A CANDLE HE'D BE NAMED AMARETTO EXPLOSION OR MOCHA ANGEL

I WANT JULIAN TO BE A CANDLE

SO I CAN TAKE HIM HOME

IT IS FIVE MINUTES FROM CLOSING TIME, I DROVE HERE AFTER THERE WAS NOTHING ON TELEVISION, MY SON EATING HIS DINNER IN HIS ROOM, ME PICKING UP THE PHONE AND PUTTING IT BACK DOWN, ME SITTING ON MY PORCH TO WATCH THE SUN SET, THE SUN MELTING LIKE THE DISCONTINUED PSYCHEDELIC SHERBET LINE

I DROVE HERE I CAN'T HELP IT

BEACH SANDALS SMELLS LIKE THE DIRT ROAD ME AND THE BOY PULLED OVER ON

I CAN'T HELP IT

I WAS A HOT BITCH IN MY DAY BUT NOW I AM SHAPED LIKE A CANDLE

DISHES

At breakfast my kid practices his ABCs and barfs into his cereal bowl just before Q. My other kid points out how the barf splashed onto the table in the shape of Oklahoma. I don't tell him it looks more like Texas, he's a little kid and if he wants to mistake Texas for Oklahoma it's no skin off my tit. My husband wipes up the barf and I watch his shorts bunch in his ass.

Before I leave for work my kid hands me a brown bag and tells me he's made my lunch, when I'm halfway down the driveway he yells after me, Big girls gotta eat! and I guess I taught him that saying, it's what I usually say when I'm eating in front of other people, because I am a big girl, that's a fact, and it makes people feel better if it's acknowledged. I give my kid a thumbs-up and oink like a pig, he loves it, standing in the doorway in his undies, doubled over.

Backing down the driveway I roll over the front wheel of my kid's bike, but he doesn't see, he'd gone back inside, the dog in the doorway now, the puddle eyes in that box head watching me balefully.

At the light I eat what's in the brown bag, a Fruit Roll-Up and seven Tootsie Rolls, a half-drunk juice box, the single Goldfish cracker way down at the bottom.

At work a lady wants her hair to look exactly like a bowl of Trix. The girl next to me helps a lady who wants hair the exact shade of maple syrup. Rich, she tells the girl, rich and lustrous. In the back we laugh at her, mime rubbing our nipples in the heat of climax, saying, Lllllustrous! A man with a glass eye tells me his hair used to be more pepper but he was glad for the salt, it's distinguished, I nick the pink mole on his neck but he doesn't notice. A girl comes in asking for red Kool-Aid hair but it comes out more like orange Triaminic, she doesn't seem to care, some people like being ugly I guess.

Later on I trim the waxer's bangs and in return she waxes my bikini line. Hold this back, she says, pushes up on my belly fat, layered blobs of tapioca pudding. Big girls gotta eat, I say, and the waxer laughs, holds her legs together like she might pee. You are too funny, she says, you are just too funny. Breathes in deep, rips the strips of paper, holds them up to show me, pube Fruit Roll-Ups. See all that nasty hair we got? See all those roots? Next time we'll do your arms.

At lunch we have pizza, someone's client is the manager at the Pizza Slab. For a snack we order wings from the bar next door. I alternate celery stick, wing, celery stick, wing. We smoke out back, a while ago someone wrote, You so ugly on the seat of the one chair out there, it's a badge of courage to sit in the ugly chair, the pedicurist declaring me so ugly that I could scare the shit out of poop. Everyone laughs and me the hardest, when she's not looking I ash into the pedicurist's side part, go back inside.

My husband calls, the TV blaring in the background. Could I pick up some laundry detergent he asks, could I also pick up some beer, something for dinner, dessert, breakfast, lunch for the rest of the week, juice. What are you watching? I ask him. The History channel, he says, but I know better, I hear the childlike yelling of those anime cartoons he loves, I know he is at half-chub and doesn't want to talk about it, I hang up over him saying, And some string cheeses.

At the grocery store a song about a man on a boat is playing, he feels so free. I stand in the frozen foods aisle, all the boxes are green or red, stop and go, yes and no, I get raviolis and frozen peas and chicken nuggets and a cheesecake. At the checkout I add two packs of bubble gum, the kids will probably chew three times and swallow just like always. A tabloid shows a young starlet's cottage cheese thighs. I ask the cashier to wait while I run to the dairy aisle, I am craving cottage cheese now, I get the biggest tub there is, large curd, I laugh to myself, I laugh and laugh, big girls gotta eat. In the car I listen to a song about a small-town slut, the DJ comes on and assures me there's more where that came from, a song about a lonely desert wanderer starts, I pass tacos pizzas chicken ice cream barbecue. The sky is pink meatblood, is a runny sorbet, the sun is a melting butterscotch, the sky is a dirty plate.

NIXON IN RETIREMENT

I had an egg for breakfast. I put too much salt on it so Pat would notice and yell at me. She didn't. Sipped her coffee like it was tea. Smiled like the machine of her mouth was winding down. A bit of hair had come loose from its setting. Like she was molting. I was grateful to see her flawed, I can't tell you exactly why. That egg was like eating a jellyfish coated in sand. I endured. The last time I was at the beach a teenaged girl walked over. She was fully developed, I don't mind telling you. Mr. Nixon, she said. Not President Nixon, or Mr. President. Mr. Nixon. I could try to forgive her for that but who has the time? Her voice was like a cartoon squirrel's. Some moptop future Democrat might like to climb all over her. I held it together. I just wanted to come over and see if it was really you, the girl squeaked. In the flesh, I answered her.

The truth was I could feel every inch of my flesh, even the dark catacombs in my trousers. Could have been the sun. Could have been the girl. Could have been any girl from the neck to the upper thigh. Wow, the girl said. Just wow! Super, was my reply. Whitehead, my day man, cleared his throat. Oh, the girl said. Is this your Secret Service man? If I told you that, I said, he'd have to kill you. I winked up at her. I was wearing sunglasses. No way she saw. I had said the wrong thing, it was clear. The girl went stiff, like she'd been flashed in ice. Could have chipped pieces of her for my drink. And all right, I would have chosen her breasts. Two breasts floating in a tumbler of Scotch, softening with melt into goosepimpled skin. That's what I call a Saturday. The girl chopped at the sand with her feet, walking backward. Thanks for your interest, I called to her. Her body a ripple of movement. From ice to jelly. Jiggling, you understand. I looked at Whitehead, that block. He looked around, turning in a slow circle. Good man. The girl had vanished, absorbed into the landscape before me, a landscape owned and operated by teenagers. The world's future leaders. My ulcers went zap. Instead of landscape perhaps I should say channel, should say program. All of them playing a part, all of them in Technicolor. Was there any real dialogue to be had, anymore? My God, what a boredom.

Pat took my plate, clacked it to the sink. Clacked back to me. Kissed my cheek. She smelled like the air in a forgotten trunk filled with flowers. I smelled it with my throat, in other words. Words burbled forth from the pink, oiled relief of her lips. That misplaced feather of hair fluttered near her ear. Pat, I wanted to say. Pat! Time is a thing that moves. We are not the ones moving. Back in our early days in the White House I had once balanced her on my lap in the tub. We were nearly sixty. She'd come back from some dinner drunk, my favorite Pat. We went to the bath, we made a froth. Two men waited outside the door. You learned not to care about such things. Later Pat lurched from bed, upchucked into the gold wastebasket. I put her back to bed, handed the wastebasket to one of the men outside the door. In the morning I gave a televised speech. You beautiful citizens, I wanted to say, is there anything more important than having your wife in whatever room you choose? If there had been an amendment guaranteeing such a right, I'd have ratified it then and there. Instead I continued with my speech. Often, I wished for a lever that would allow me to send an electric current from my desk to every citizen's home. I wish for that still. Did you hear me, Richie? Pat asked. Sure, I said. There came the lips. Other cheek, kissed. I palmed her breast. It was as loose and lifeless as a chicken cutlet. She didn't notice. Clacked out the door. Her ass these days was still tight in her white pants, but was the shape of two halved apples. An old woman's ass. Her day man followed a polite three steps behind.

•••

Late morning, nine holes with an old lobbyist friend. After lunch, nap. During nap, I'll do my damnedest to enter my favorite dream, the dream in which I've mounted Jackie Kennedy on the steps of my alma mater. It's a cold night and we are under my coat. The stars are like flecks of ice on a dark ocean. After nap, dinner with Pat. After dinner, telephone hour. After telephone hour, bed. Pat calls our bedroom the Secret Garden. Because of all the florals. Like we are preparing for the casket. Tonight I will reach for my wife the way I reach for Jackie in that dream. Like I mean it. Not open to discussion. It's not Jackie Kennedy that is the draw. It is that in the dream neither of us has seen the inside of the White House. We are just two people getting primitive. History corrected. I can taste it like a brine: so many mistakes. Tonight I want to touch Pat. See her the way she was. Skin like cream, bright bright eyes. Present corrected. Forget how the world has turned on its axis for all of eternity. And will long after I'm gone.

DALLAS

Dallas's momma kicked him out three nights before. He slept the first two nights next to the old man next door on a yellowed twin mattress. The bed was up on cinder blocks and the old man used their hollow centers to display his valuables, which looked to be made up mostly of chipped chess pieces and dinged-up model cars and pink bunches of toilet paper Dallas guessed were supposed to look like paper flowers, or something. The old man was out on his porch when Dallas's momma chased him out the house with his own switchblade, and soon as she slammed the door the old man waved Dallas over with his old-man claw, said, They's biscuits and jam and shit in the kitchen, help yeself. The old man had cable, and besides Dallas wasn't a snob or anything, if the old man needed someone's arm to hold at night Dallas wasn't fixing to call the authorities over it, except during the third night the old man tried to roll over onto Dallas, whispering about how Dallas could have anything in the house, money, things worth money, even that guitar in the corner, and Dallas at first just let it happen, he couldn't quite catch up to why there should be any bother with it, and then something surged up in his gut, something tentacled, and he pushed the man off him and ran out the house with his pants and shoes in one hand and the guitar in the other, and then when his bare feet hit the cold grass in the yard he thought maybe how that was the first time he'd ever actively decided he didn't want something to happen, and he wondered if that meant he was a man, at least according to what his momma would think was a man. He looked toward his momma's house, could see the light from the TV in the front room through the curtains, his momma just inside relaxing and enjoying herself with a glass of beer resting comfortably on that big whale belly while he looked longingly in, her own son shirtless, and Dallas put on his pants and shoes and walked past her house and the one after that and then the one after that, and he turned a corner and walked all the way to the park and slept in the soft dirt under the monkey bars. In the morning a redheaded child stood over him and asked him could he please move, she was trying to practice. The sky was the color of the buttermilk his momma drank every morning and it hurt his eyes. He sat on a swing and watched the child for a while. She pumped her legs and grunted. The guitar wasn't anywhere his eyes could see and he tried to work up some emotion about that but there was none.

He walked over and asked the child for some change. She stopped moving and hung there, arms straight. Her hair shimmered in defiance of such an ugly sky. For a minute Dallas saw friendship in her big child's eyes, and he felt his heart open a little, like a blossom, or a fist, then she told him, Take yeself to a shirt store, you all burnt up, then take yeself to a churchly place where you could find a bath. Dallas said, No one likes a redhead anyway, and grownups don't bathe, they shower, and then he stuck his fingers in her pockets and fished out a nickel and a dime and a colorless gumball he popped immediately into his mouth. In the scuffle the child dropped down and fell to her knees and let loose a warbling cry Dallas recognized as mostly anger, and he turned and ran. After a few blocks he slowed and spit the gum at his feet, kept spitting every few steps because it felt appropriate. Yessir, he said as loud as he pleased, just *exactly* like a fist.

Dallas knew there was a Circle K a few streets over and he walked there to pass some time. Inside he loitered in the home-aids aisle and pretended to be choosing between two different types of lightbulbs. When the girl at the counter wasn't looking he snatched a shirt with *Who*

Farted? printed on it and put it on inside out. He moved to the soda machine and cupped his hand under the orange Fanta and helped himself while the girl tended to the donut case. Dallas watched a man survey the candy selection at the counter. After a while he settled on a packet of licorice rope and some Goobers. Dallas walked over and said, I'll give you fifteen cents for a lift to wherever you going, and without meeting Dallas's eye the man said, Surely can, I'm a Christian ain't I?

Dallas rode in the cab of the man's truck. It felt like afternoon but he couldn't be sure. That odd sky lay above him like a yellowed sheet but quite a breeze got worked up and whipped around him and through his hair and it was all Dallas could do not to open his mouth and swallow up big mouthfuls of it. The truck slowed and turned and Dallas saw that the man was going to the movies. He wondered what kind of man this was, going to a movie in the middle of the day, but he was grateful to arrive at some kind of destination.

The man got out and shoved the candy packages down the back of his pants. He looked toward Dallas, but the tint in his glasses made it near impossible to tell whether Dallas was being looked at. You can come along, the man said, should you desire to. The man had a cleft lip but Dallas realized a movie sounded like just the thing, and he jumped from the cab and followed the man inside.

The man bought two tickets and when Dallas paused by the snack counter, near bloodthirsty for a kernel of popcorn or a pat of butter, the man slapped his leg like a master to his dog. Dallas choked back a robust Fuck you and followed the man into the pleasant darkness of the theater. You sit down here, the man whispered, pointing to a row in the middle. I'm up there, he said, and we ain't together from here on out. The man turned and Dallas watched him trudge up the steps, holding his pants where he'd stuffed the packets of candy. The rest of the theater was empty so Dallas chose him a seat where he pleased relative to the area the man in the glasses allowed him.

Dallas hoped this was a movie with some kind of monster or evil snake or something. At least featuring knives and guns or a tank or a ghost. Then when the lights came all the way down Dallas couldn't tell what kind of movie it was. A woman looked out and didn't say nothing. A man in a suit started his car, then sat there. A few strings were plucked for musical effect. Dallas got a feeling that he tried to laugh off, a feeling like the light coming from the screen was a spotlight on him, like the movie was watching him rather than the other way around, only he didn't have no story to tell. Suddenly the man in the glasses came down the steps and walked out the door marked EXIT, slamming the door behind him. Dallas was alone and the woman in the film was walking toward a door in a hallway. Dallas didn't want to see the other side of that door and he'd be damned if he was going to sit and figure out why. He ran and burst out the exit. He saw he was at the back of the building and the man in the glasses was gone.

A lady in a wheelchair was sitting near a propped-open door, smoking. Dallas recognized her as one of the ticket takers. She squinted at Dallas, called over, Ain't that movie a bore? Her legs looked shriveled inside her pants. He wondered if she could hear the same buzz he heard, like a thousand voices and a clump of cicadas and a steady rain. He wondered if things shimmered when she looked at them as they did for him. He wondered if she felt like her insides were on her outsides all the time like he did. The woman opened her mouth and let the smoke meander out. She seemed content to just watch him and let him watch her. He realized if he wanted to he could walk over and start to love this woman. He imagined waking up and making toast in her yellow kitchen, patting her cat between its ears, reading the TV guide to her each night.

But then it seemed such a long distance to walk, from his exit to hers, and instead Dallas nodded his head at her and walked off toward the highway, another sound. He walked up an entrance ramp headed west, keeping to the shoulder and thinking of his momma and the cold cuts she always had in the icebox, and he decided right then to get off at the next exit and go home, but it seemed like something he wanted to do more than anything he would ever actually be able to do, and then the sun was setting and the sky finally colored and so Dallas walked first toward a horizon colored orange, and then pink, and then blue, and then a man driving a semi slowed and pulled over and offered Dallas a ride, and by then the lights on the highway had come on and he couldn't see the sky no more anyway, the semi picking up speed and the man whistling a tune and Dallas putting his hand on the man's thigh because he was hungry enough to eat his own arm or anything that was offered to him from that moment on.

GERALD'S WIFE

The smell of lumber. Bits of wood in the air. Golden motes. The day of the funeral, a stream of light through the curtains. Dust twirling like glitter. Bitsy from next door saying, She never was much of a housekeeper. Skin of a raisin on her front tooth.

You need something cut, my friend? Gerald shook his head. The wood was a comfort but he had to move on.

Aisle of shovels. Something with a handle, ain't too heavy. Might as well pay the extra two dollars.

Lantern? Flashlight. Years ago they'd gone camping. Gerald backed over the flashlight they'd bought special.

Deirdre made a quiet noise with her tongue. Gerald had wanted to yell.

Lantern. Deirdre reading in bed, making those *mmm* noises. Like each word was a revelation. Every now and again she'd leave that lamp on all night.

The day she died, the blown bulb. Flick, nothing. Flick, nothing. The gray bulb, the broken filament. Deirdre's crumpled arm. The brown wet at the seat of her pants, the small pool of bile. Milk-clouded eyes. Stroke, the doctor said. Her brain broke, was how Gerald would tell it. Cloudy bulb eyes, broken filament brain.

Lightbulbs? Gerald said it aloud, said it toward the aproned black woman limping toward him. Her hand crumpled at her ribs. Mouth wet at one corner. Broke brain, Gerald thought.

Aisle thirteen, came the answer. Clear as a bell. All fixed up. Crescent wrench, x-ray, level. Scalpel, spade. Hard to know where to start. We had to break Deirdre's hips, the man at the funeral home said. So her legs'd fit right. Obligated to let you know. In the casket the little finger she broke in the fall angled up, dainty as a princess.

Aisle thirteen. Only Gerald couldn't bring himself. Didn't seem like the right fix.

Ax. Crowbar? Better safe than sorry. Deirdre had wanted a gun. Better safe than sorry, she said. Phone call from the range. Your gun's ready, the man said. Come in anytime with a certified check. Hard to shoot when you're already dead, Gerald told him. The man laughed. He had a brown tooth, Gerald remembered. Fit his laugh, laugh like a lungful of brown teeth. Rev rev rev whee.

All you're forgetting's your tarp! Chubby girl, curls hair-sprayed to her forehead. You're committing the perfect murder, right? Chubby smile. Chubby fist at her hip. All that flesh, so much flesh.

Yeah, get me one, Gerald told her. A blue one and some bungees. I don't want clear.

Chubby face held tight. Quiet call on her walkie. Old man, smeared rose tattoo on his arm. This all right?

Seventy-four twenty-eight. Twenty-eight how old Deirdre was when they married. Deirdre whispered, Lucky you, I ain't wearing no panties, right there at the altar. Turned out a lie. Minister sweating slick fat drops and all for nothing.

Deirdre always did like to lie.

Whoosh went the doors. Whoosh went the heat. Store climate-controlled as a coffin. Gerald rushed his purchases into the trunk. Safe in there, sealed like a tomb. Coffin, tomb. Beats of his heart. Coff-in, tomb tomb. Coff-in, tomb tomb.

You're being dramatic. Deirdre's sister. Hair in a froth. Throat asparkle. Nails like a hawk's. Swoop, Move on. Swoop, I always did find you manly. Swoop, wet lozenge, nest on a napkin. Swoop, bloodstained beak. Swoop, Gerald played dead. Gerald refused to writhe.

There went the sun. Quick as a cookie into milk. Nothing on the radio. Man promising there'd be something soon, throat like a cave. Gerald agreed.

Deirdre buried way back. Newest part, the man at the funeral home had declared. Deandra got the place all to herself, he said. Didn't mention the stick trees bent like burnt orphans. Didn't mention they ain't built the walkway that far yet. And then Gerald hating to mention how he'd rearrange the man's acorns should the stone say Deandra and not Deirdre.

Passion, Deirdre would hiss. All I'm asking for. Gerald grabbed, one hand for the tit, one hand for the warmth down between her legs. That wasn't it, turned out. That was far from it. A PASSIONITE WOMAN, the stone said.

Park the car. Throw the tools over. Climb. Climb down. Gerald nothing but a list now, lines on his skin, pencil in the lines.

Deirdre hands in the sink. Deirdre sweaty hair at her neck. Deirdre clap, smeared red of a mosquito. Deirdre in her yellow robe, feet bottoms black as coal. Deirdre Ain't you going to let me in? Deirdre mmm. Deirdre mmm. Deirdre ding, Deirdre dong, Deirdre How's a girl supposed to breathe in heat like this? Soapy water, smell of soap. Thread of dirt, black black smell.

Three months buried. Chiff went the shovel. Grass like a carpet. Dry soil, all burnt up. Chiff. Chiff. Chiff. If I ever die, don't bury me. Denim-blue night. Burn me up, feed me to the pigs, throw me over tied to an anchor. Train whistle, baying dog, smell of rain. Okay? Okay?

Chiff. Deirdre's hand, cold as a cooler. Mind the pinky.

Just dreams! Deirdre's sister, feather of lipstick on her incisor. She's dead!

Day of the funeral, throat shoveled raw. Fart, went Bitsy. Gerald turned to nudge Deirdre. Oh, he said. Oh, that's right. Oh, he kept saying. Shh, now, came all the replies. Shh.

And here she'd been, to think. Ninety-two days bored and hot. Chiff. Married thirty-three years, a prophet's lifetime. Can't escape that easy!

Gerald in up to his shoulders now. Chiff. Sun at his neck like a slap. Shovel to wood, a stop. Stop went the shovel. Go went the ax.

Help you? Wet voice of a boy.

Pow went the ax. Came apart in his hands. Funeral man saying, Nothing's coming through this sucker, not no maggots and not no ghosts. Rev rev whee. Chain saw? Gerald asked the boy.

Come out from there. Sanded voice of a man. Gerald looked up. Sky boy man. Sky like the water in a tub. Chain saw, Gerald said. Deirdre and all this nothing to look at.

Can't help you there, came the man. Time to come on out from there.

Dirt on his tongue. She's in there. Dirt in his eyes.

That ain't her no more, said the man.

All that dirt in her breaths. Deirdre and the candy pink of her toenails. Deirdre and them dirty feet. Tiptoeing across the porch just the night before. Ruined blade in his hands, shimmering useful as a fish. Gerald at the chipped white kitchen table, night after night these ninety-two days. Crackers cheese beer, all that silence and chewing, the television and its noises. Loneliness a nightly death, bed a burial. All this dirt, all that wood. The sound of her voice, even that gone? Gerald's cremated heart, Gerald's aching burned-up heart. Nothing but urn left now. Gerald meaning to say, She's alive and she can't breathe, thinking how most of the time he hated her, that mean mouth, he missed that hate, its absence a hacked-up emptiness, Gerald meaning to say, She's alive and she can't breathe, Gerald saying, I'm alive and I can't breathe.

ME AND GIN

Me and Gin play Lips. This a game where you see how long you can touch lips before you need to scream. Gin always the one screaming first, I guess not always, sometimes I scream first cause I don't want to seem like no weird lips lover.

Me and Gin's both girls. See.

Me and Gin go over each other's houses, mostly hers though, cause my daddy don't like wearing shirts always, and Gin says he got flabby baby boobs, and when I tell Daddy this he cups what he got and says, That bitch just can't handle her fiery attraction, and I laugh cause it seems like the right thing to do, and Daddy digs out the last of the Skoal and places it tenderly.

Me and Gin decided it ain't cool to call each other bitch. I nod and nod at her, I want her to know I agree, but inside I am forlorn, I will have to find another word that sounds so powerful. Bitch like a bull stamping its hooves, bitch like a broom after a crow.

Me and Gin got to agree on things, cause she's my first friend and I got to hold on tight.

Me and Gin like to play preacher and supplicant, Gin is always the preacher and I am always the supplicant. Gin saying, You a fearful sinner, young lady, and me heaving my shoulders, begging, Please. I never say what I'm pleasing for, just Please, please.

Sometimes Gin slaps me in the head and I fall and wriggle, watching the pink blades of her ceiling fan with my boggled eyes, I am consumed with the power of her touch, least I think that's what I'm doing, other times Gin'll say, All right, cause that means she's done and I need to be done too.

Me and Gin hold hands in the movies, practicing, till a fat lady sits in our row.

Me and Gin had a fight once, when I came upon her sitting on my brother's bed like she does on mine. And my brother just tiddling with his football, poke arms sticking out his muscle shirt like creamy bone. Gin and my brother, talking like they was afraid of the sound. And me wanting to say, Hold up, this is mine and this is mine, I almost said it, but I didn't, cause no one likes to be claimed. Instead I said, Guess I'll go to the bathroom now, and I did, and I looked at my face in the mirror so long I got so I couldn't recognize it.

Me and Gin made up and she let me wear her hair clip for the afternoon.

Me and Gin like to ride our bikes out to the Circle K. I get Gin a Faygo and me a Yoo-hoo and this one time at the last second I add a six-pack of lightbulbs, a treat for Gin, she don't know what joy she in for. We ride a few blocks and then I say, Okay, Gin, time to stop. Then I show her what I mean, I get me a lightbulb and place it on the ground and then I whomp on it with both feet, the sound, the sound, the God-loving crunch. Now you, I tell Gin, but she ain't smiling like I am, and she don't take the lightbulb from my hand. Have fun cleaning that up, Gin says, and goes after her kickstand with a fury that makes her miss it the first try. I didn't mean to, I call after her, cause this is what you supposed to say in a apology situation, but Gin don't look back. But see I did mean to, how could I not?

Me and Gin decide she is right, we are too old and feminine for stomping anything into dust. Gin's momma makes us graham crackers and butter, Gin licking the butter off with the tip of her tongue, I say, No, thanks, I ate a healthy lunch, which is a lie.

Me and Gin talk about what we going to wear the first day of school, I pretend to think about it and say, I believe I will wear my jean shorts and a T-shirt. I don't have no other options, cause Daddy says we got to make do with what we have, 'less clothes rain from the sky that is, and that is A-OK by me, I like my shorts. But Gin is disappointed, her face a curdled pie, so I add, And some cherry lip chap, and this does the trick.

Me and Gin. That is fun to say, it is right, it is a joyful clump of words. Me and Gin is forever, we planets, everything outside us all but a darkness.

Me and Gin say we best get the same classes or else, cause we is best friends and nothing can change that. I say, Yep, we blood brothers, cause it is nighttime and I'm in my sleeping bag on her floor and it is like the night sky burbling stars is inside me, but Gin says, We ain't boys, and we don't mess with blood, and this is a disappointment, but I let it pass, I pretend to sleep, I don't tell Gin how our blood glitters, how we half light, I keep all that to myself.

OUR MAN

THE SISTER:

Don't worry, I said. This will hurt, and then it won't. Or go ahead and worry, I said, if that's the kind of person you are.

THE DETECTIVE:

What am I here for, if the crime's been solved?

First you hafta name the crime.

Easy: murder.

That's only the beginning, Detective Tin Ears.

One of those.

One of those. Better you than me. I've got enough blood on my hands.

I'll start with the scene.

When you find out where that is, you let me know.

Women.

Women.

THE SISTER:

How about this: a man bleeds in velvety ribbons. Our man is a teapot with two spouts. His heart is still intact, if that's what you're worried about. (His heart is the problem.) Our man bleeds blackly, redly, deadly. Our man was gone in a few great gushes. I'm a collector and I came to.

It's me. You can be you. I've been honest and I'm being honest now. Blood is just as thick as we've heard. Blood doesn't cool if you admit relief. That rust-colored pump will throb on and on.

Somebody tarred Daddy to the floor.

I can't deny it's gorgeous that a brain sees what its

THE DETECTIVE:

The detective set out. Squeezed the last bits of whiskey from the Ziploc he kept in his breast pocket. The road unfurled in the white wash from his headlights. He had her underwear in his fist, damp with blood, and when he held them to his mouth he smelled iron, or something that should be called iron. Perhaps it really was a man's blood.

When they found her, two severed ears were gripped in her bloodslick hands. She declined the offer to hand them over. She was naked except for the underwear. A lady cop was called in to cuff her.

The detective held his breath driving past the

experience has trained it to see. If you've never known love it's clear you'd mistake it for something else. Loneliness perhaps. Greed.

How about: blood congeals and forms a skin. Or: our man's dying breath lasted fifteen seconds. This: we both love(d) you more than life itself.

cemetery, pushing the panties into his mouth just short of gagging.

THE WIFE:

I was born with an extra spine in a lump on my shoulder. My parents had it removed but I can still feel it. Like a ghost limb. Like a ghost twin. She grew up and lived and she weighs me down and we share everything. My parents called her Imaginary Friend. Sometimes it's just too hard to relate to the real thing. None of this is true, of course. It's just the easiest way to explain.

Of course none of this is true. I'll try another way. There was a girl that died mysteriously down the street when I was growing up. After her funeral I saw her white face in her bedroom window, watching me, mouthing, Wait for me, wait for me, and I waited

THE SISTER:

Oh, and the way he'd kiss me. Like I was you. Like I was the you he always dreamed I was. If you are discourteous with a rose its petals will bruise. That's how he kissed me, so gorgeously discourteously. I could feel my heart beating in my lips. I could feel the throb of blood.

and I'm still waiting. Every once in a while I hear her name being called, but there's never an answer.

No. No. No. No.

Here: her room was across the hall. At night I stood outside her door and listened for her breathing but I couldn't hear anything over the roar of silence. I watched her chest not move. She was dead and then the morning would come and she was alive. There was no way she could die. There was no way she could be revived. We wrote notes to each other and slid them under our doors. Mine said, I wish I was alone. Hers said, I miss you.

THE DETECTIVE:

The detective stopped at a do-it-yourself car wash. Got out and leaned against the car, did a few toots of Afrin. The lights hummed and a hot moist wind came in and made his neck sweat. He'd punched in three hours and forty-seven minutes ago. He had four hours and thirteen minutes to go. He had to be looking for something.

Pretty soon he heard the squeaking, like a mouse caught in a trap. The lights blinded him and all he saw was a vivid darkness. He listened to her getting closer.

Then she was there, squinting up at him from the edge between light and dark. A child's head, the cherubic

A JOKE, PUNCH LINE FORTHCOMING:

Once there was a man who wanted to build his wife the house of her dreams. He began working for a contractor, building other people's houses, and each day he'd steal a brick, hiding it under his shirt or in his lunch pail and bringing it home. On his final day the contractor caught him. Please, the man said. This is the last brick I need to complete my house. I'll do anything for that brick. Well, the contractor said, I'm going to throw it up as high as it'll go, and if you can catch that brick it's yours and I won't come after you for the others. The man agreed that it was a fair proposition. The contractor took a few steps back, face, the purple empty gums, the wisps of hair. The body of a trucker, its puffed, sexless chest, its clumpy limbs. The wheelchair and the mangled hands forcing its wheels along. The drool bright on her chin. The smell of urine and cinnamon chewing gum. The MacGuffin.

She motioned to the Afrin and he gave it to her. He was glad for the other one he had in the glove compartment.

Pretty soon he couldn't smell the urine anymore. He got used to it. She wheeled away and he figured that meant follow. He figured he had to start somewhere.

breathed deeply, and flung the brick high. The sun flashed behind it. The man's heart pounded desperately.

THE DETECTIVE:

The detective began to feel the effects of the whiskey and Afrin. He put a few gobs of Vicks under his nostrils and talked to himself in the rearview. A man is dead, we can all agree on that. Count to ten. One. Two. Three. Four. Five. Six. Oh hell. Ten. Remember that God and murder are in the details. He noticed that the area around his mouth was a bit pink from the bloody underwear. He got stern. You're makin me sick. Stop talkin to yourself and get out there and do it. The Vicks made his eyes water.

The MacGuffin squeaked along in front of him. The tears in his eyes and the headlights smeared every-

THE WIFE:

In my opinion she couldn't tell she existed. That's why she does it (did it) to us.

He had a tattoo of a heart over his heart because he said that's how he knew where he ended and we began.

I still have those notes. I wonder if she kept mine. Oh God, all that blood? Is he a ghost now? Is he a white face in a window? Were we married?

thing and he lost her. He circled back to the office so he could start again, retrace his steps.

THE SISTER:

We love(d) you more than all the bricks in Brooklyn.

THE DETECTIVE:

If this is tedious to you, Tin Ears, there's a desk job with your name on it.

Murder's tedious.

That's just a label. We got a ransom letter. Prints all over it. Pubic hair taped in a circular clump—looks like it might be the point of the exclamation point.

Cripes. What's it say. (come on come on)

Search me. I don't read shouting. Bad for the eyes. Jameson, read it to me.

And.

It says if you want the body you'll have to kill for it.

That doesn't make any sense.

It makes perfect sense, Tin Ears. Perfect sense.

What's it askin.

It's asking you to produce the body. No body no death.

THE SISTER:

Dearest love, let me count the ways. Dismemberment, garroted, poisoned, drowned, named. I read that as soon as a species is named it begins its travels up the endangered list. Discovery meaning death.

He *asked* me to cut him. I did. The blood, disappointingly, did not drip. It seeped. We gathered it with a tiny blue washcloth.

THE CORPSE:

Ahem. I believe I've earned the right to step in here. At least as some kind of oxymoronic metaphor for this plus this equals that. The dimple in my tie filled with blood. I was wived and I made my wife a widow. And is this really me speaking? Am I being imagined?

Somebody tarred Daddy to the floor. My ears splitting, off they went.

THE DETECTIVE:

The detective took the letter down to run its prints, find out if the pubic hair was of the male or female persuasion. He held its corner with red tweezers and it flapped along beside him. Smith cut out the whole exclamation point with an X-Acto knife and his eyes got round at all that possible DNA. He said, Hopefully there's a root or two. His breath smelled like onions. The detective's stomach turned. Jenny took the letter minus the exclamation point and promised to dust for prints before her shift ended. The detective noted her waves of red hair and the mole just under her nose and decided one didn't cancel out the other.

THE SISTER:

If there's anything we've learned it's that roses are red. I planted our man, told him the eyes are the last to go, and he believed me. Our man bloomed and died and a year later bloomed again. That's the hope anyway. And did you know that a human head weighs more than the shovel.

Dearest, you say you understand, but if you did you'd stop crying.

We had a child. Our man named him Junior. Our man thought it was all a dream until it actually became a dream, and then he knew how real it was. And did you know blood tastes sweet like summer grass.

On his way out to the car his nostrils started closing in on him. He opened the glove compartment so fast the Afrin bounced under the seat and he cursed. The body, the Afrin, he'd have to reach for both. He didn't know why he had to look for something that wasn't even hiding.

THE DETECTIVE:

Knuckles rapped on the window. The detective rolled it down and smoke poured in from the chief's pipe.

She's confessed again, he said, squinting. You better beat it.

The detective nodded, began rolling up the window, and the chief stepped back.

I'm on it, the detective said through the glass. The car started too smoothly. He had three hours and seven minutes left on his shift. He drove due south, fast. There was a truck stop he knew of where he could be alone and eat. There had to be.

THE CORPSE:

This is how I imagined being dead:

Idon'tknow Idon'tknow
Idon'tknow Idon'tknow
Idon'tknow Idon'tknow
Idon'tknow Idon'tknow
Idon'tknow Idon'tknow
Idon'tknow Idon'tknow
Idon'tknow Idon'tknow
Idon'tknow Idon'tknow
Idon'tknow Idon'tknow
Idon'tknow Idon'tknow
Idon'tknow Idon'tknow
Idon'tknow Idon'tknow
Idon'tknow
andIdon'tcaretoknow.

Hard to know where you are if everyone who knows you doesn't know where you are and if the one who loves you most will never come looking for you. I'm here. I'm pointing at myself. My heart is sort of beating.

THE WIFE:

When we got married I told myself when he's dead I'll know it immediately. But I still can't convince myself he was ever alive in the first place. Absence makes the heart grow fonder of absence. I shave my legs with his razor. Blood shimmies. It was always my razor.

A JOKE, PART TWO:

So this lady is in first class, real snooty-looking broad, and she's got this poodle in her lap that yaps with practically every breath. Next to her is this real salt-of-the-earth-type guy, like the kind of guy who starts from nothing and ends up richer than anything. So the guy says to the lady, Look, you gotta shut that dog up and the lady takes offense and says, My dog is no worse than your disgusting cigar smoke. And they go back and forth like that and it starts to get ugly. So the guy says, Fine, lady, you asked for it, and he takes the poodle and throws it out the emergency-exit window. The lady is downright astonished, and she yanks the cigar out of the guy's mouth and throws it out the window too. Well this makes them both laugh and they become great friends, and when they land, the guy says he'll help the lady find her poodle, he's real sorry, and the lady says no, she's sorry, and they set out together. So they find the poodle wandering around this field in a daze, and guess what it's got in its mouth?

THE PUNCH LINE:

The brick.

THE DETECTIVE:

The truck stop said OPEN in green letters. The detective wiped his neck with the underwear and put it back in his pocket. Inside, he ordered coffee and creamed wheat and watched the cook scratch his armpit. The waitress had a peanut shell in her hair. The jukebox played something country-sounding, of course it did, and it seemed to be on repeat.

The detective's head pulsed. When the waitress turned he tooted some Afrin and nearly cried. When she came back with his coffee he plucked the peanut shell from her hair and handed it to her. Thank you, she said, and she looked touched.

The detective stuck his finger in the coffee and stirred. A woman came out of the ladies' and sat at the other end of the counter. She watched him from the corner of her eye and then she said, Sir, you are unpleasant.

The detective was startled. He threw a ten on the counter and walked out and the night was cool. He purposely mistook the city lights for stars.

He went to his car and grabbed the cuffs. Back inside the cook had his chin on his forearms and seemed to be lost in thought. Okay, the detective said, let's go. Get up.

The woman at the end of the counter didn't move so the detective got rough with her. He mostly yelled. The waitress wiped the counter in slow circles. The woman's shoes were loud on the floor and louder on the gravel outside. The detective threw her in the backseat. You're gonna talk, he hissed, and you're gonna say what I want you to say. The woman's eyes glittered meanly.

The detective slammed the car door and went back in for his creamed wheat. Only then did he hear the bell over the door, violent with jingling.

THE SISTER CONFESSES:

I said, This is going to hurt. I said, If you insist on being so quiet I'll be forced to make you scream. I said, You can't love we but we can love you.

The shears—or was it a razor?

The blade. The blade looked like a blade and cut like a blade. It happened how it should.

Our man's eyes were a thin shade of blue. We mashed teeth when we kissed. If you see my sister tell her to give me a ring.

THE DETECTIVE:

The chief's cigar dangled. Put her in a lineup with the others, he said.

THE WIFE CONFESSES:

Listen. She thinks I'm not listening. If she says he's dead he's probably dead. When we were young we buried things.

We've got a man on the case.

THE DETECTIVE:

The detective thought about smudging:

Description: earless body, man, blood

into his fogged windshield. The woman in the backseat whined. The highway drifted on and the detective got bored with counting lights.

Tell me, the detective said.

When I was twenty I fell in love with a houseplant, she said. When I was fifteen I murdered my mother's fancy soaps. She said, I've always hated shells. Something about the shape.

The detective noted the gap in her front teeth, the brass in her hair. Maybe,

THE CORPSE:

I said a lot of things I didn't mean.

he said, it's the halving you hate.

The woman rolled onto her back and kicked the window.

The detective shook the Afrin bottle. The familiar swish was gone. He was out. He pushed the nipple up his nose and held it there. Tell me everything, he said.

Just one last thing, she said. Her voice was low and she sniffed wetly. The truth is I'd like to go home now.

The detective smelled popcorn. Wine dregs. Something warm. She'd wet herself. I'm not buying it, he said. His patience was waning. He had one hour and forty-three minutes left.

THE WIFE AND HER SISTER:

The station boiled. Men wiped foreheads with damp handkerchiefs. Ties were loosened. In the kitchen the lone female officer pressed an icy gallon of milk to her thighs. The station pulsed. Breath was exchanged. The night wound.

The wife identified her sister. I'm ninety-nine percent sure that's her, she said.

Her sister stepped forward and bowed. Her hair cascaded in a horrible wave. Bits of it clumped with blood.

The chief blew smoke rings and shot the moon. That's our girl, he said.

THE CORPSE:

Two ears. Not even the eardrums. Cartilage, lobe. And the room bloody with blood.

The question is, is there enough of me left over for proof that I'm dead.

And should I be taking her word for it (I don't know).

THE DETECTIVE:

The detective stopped at a druggist's. Pulled the woman out by her ankles and righted her. She wobbled in and squinted under the fluorescents. Near the diapers he uncuffed her, noted her interesting bone structure. Some cheekbones, he told her.

The detective cleared the shelf of its Afrins. Turned to offer the woman a chocolate sip, but she was gone. He watched the flight of her hair. Into the dark mouth of the parking lot.

The detective got wistful, told himself she'd find her way.

The car smelled like brine and white sugar. The car smelled like her. The

THE SISTERS:

Stop crying.

I will.

You can touch me.

Where is he?

He's everywhere. He's just everywhere. Hold my hands. Feel how cold.

detective rolled down the windows and let the wind knife in. The clock said what it said.

THE SISTERS:

The sisters watched themselves. The room was silver with mirrors.

At the end of the day Jameson, the chief said, and his head was blurred in smoke, we're all just looking for ourselves. And where's Tin Ears?

The sisters held hands over the table. Their eyes locked on their eyes.

The listening room shrugged.

THE DETECTIVE:

The detective parked at the station, crawled into the back, did the Afrin. Pushed his face into the piss-filled seat. It was no longer warm. He spotted a Tootsie Roll in the floorboard and left it there. He watched Jameson walk to his car.

A small boy wrung his hands in front of the station. The detective thought how much the station looked like a yellow lightbox. The boy said, *Somebody tarred Daddy to the floor.* His eyes were small green almonds.

The detective said, Yeah, yeah, what floor? His head made bright exclamations. He could've breathed lava. He took the boy by the shoulder and pushed him into the light. He thought about the cuffs.

The fat officer at the desk eyed the boy through dark slits. The detective told the boy to have a seat. Walked back to his desk and wrote *Cheekbones* on the report. He wrote it sloppy enough so that it could be anything.

In the bathroom he ran the panties under the tap. Scrubbed his face pink. He wondered if the boy had any chalk. In the mirror he glared at himself hatefully.

THE NIGHT ENDS:

The chief said, At the end of the day, Tin Ears, the ransom note was the thing.

No body no death.

'Sright. Punch out.

Who wrote it?

Somebody else. Punch out.

THE DETECTIVE:

The detective wondered about death bloody with absence. How enough blood makes a dead man.

He took the back door. Drove a horrible length, parked at a grocery store. The day's sky was slowly spreading itself. The sun was a dazzling orange in a pool of mucus and it hurt his eyes. He had a few minutes to go before it opened. Jelly rolls. Lunch meat.

The detective thought of the boy waiting on the bench. How he might like to pick a mother out of a lineup.

He found a fresh Ziploc and some coins in the console. Anything brown would do.

THE END:

So that's it?

PLANS

I kissed a teacher once. It ain't as bad as you think. It was in Shop. He was showing me how to use the band saw and I was in the crook of his arm and we were pushing a two-by-four together and he had the windows open and there was a breeze and I just turned around and passed my tongue through his lips, easy as pie, his mouth tasted like menthol and something else, something like vinegar, something that wasn't from food or nothing, something like maybe want. Want is bitter like that is what I mean. Right after I thought of the Cheetos I had in my bag, while he looked at me from behind his dinged-up glasses, while his mouth worked like we was still at it, I just leaned back against the table and thought how I'd eat the Cheetos on the bus home, how I'd suck the orange from my fingers.

Well, he said, when his mouth finally quit.

Yep, I said. He pushed up his glasses and I could see the grit under his nails, his knuckles knobbed and leathery.

I had been planning this for a while. This man, this teacher, he was like something whittled in reverse, moving slowly back to the block. All his edges was dull, if he had any edges left. I thought about putting my hands on his belt and so I reached out and pulled at his buckle. It's easy as that if you want to know the truth. Just think something up and then do it. That's all.

He pushed at his glasses again, both hands this time, and I felt his pants get tight. All right, I told him, but he backed away and turned from me and went into his little office and closed the door.

That was that. I ain't one for pushing it. I got my stuff and wandered the halls till the bell rang and it was time to get on the bus. I ate all the Cheetos, even the little bitty ones, and I saved my fingers for last.

I thought it was funny that here I was finally with my Cheetos but all I could think about was the man's eyes behind his busted-up glasses, the nicks and scratches making his eyes look smeared and splintered, like something he would have given a low grade to: needs sanding, needs varnish, needs attention.

Anyway. There was a rough bit on my chin from where his face met mine. If you'd seen it and asked me about it, I'd have told you I fell, told you it just needed a cool cloth and some Noxzema, told you I let a football player. Cause it'd have been none of your business.

•••

I stole a coral lipstick from the grocery store while my momma was two aisles over with the frozen dinners, her hand to the glass like that's how she could read the labels. The lipstick was on a can of refried beans, still in its package, I pictured some desperate woman realizing she needed the beans more than she needed the color and placing it there when she saw no one was looking. I picked it up and worked it out of its package, a thin boy in an apron watching me from the end of the aisle, and me watching him back, me taking that lipstick out and sliding it into my jeans pocket and the boy worrying his pimpled chin with his thumb and forefinger, the boy shrugging like I had asked him and me turning to walk the other way, running my finger along the cans and boxes and bags of food cause I figured he'd be watching, but when I looked he was helping an old man reach the powdered milk and I had to touch the lipstick in my pocket to make sure I had ever been seen at all.

I wore that lipstick one night when we all met up to swim and it was so dark I let a boy take off my bottoms, the lipstick smeared and greasy all around my mouth and its crayon smell all over the boy, and then I put a ribbon on that lipstick and gave it to my momma for Christmas.

•••

I went over to a boy's house one night when my momma had the TV on so loud it rung in my teeth, so loud she didn't look up from her program when I shut the door behind me. I watched her from the window, holding her glass in the palm of her hand, flexing her toes, and if she heard me she didn't feel like doing nothing about it.

After all that loud, after all that laughter and applause and ding ding ding and welcome and good night, the quiet of the evening rushed in after it and filled me up with a fizzing, that's all I can tell you, I was all fizz and crackle and burst.

This boy went with a girlfriend of mine. But sometimes that's just tough shit.

I threw pebbles at his window till he came down, told me that was his little brother's window, told me his little brother ran and told him some queer bitch was standing in the lawn and he better do something about it.

Show me your truck, I told the boy, and we went for a drive.

The boy told me after high school he was joining up, told me his favorite food was meat loaf, told me he put the transmission in his truck all by hisself, told me he had a dream about me two nights before where I sang like a canary bird and fed him a pizza.

And then what, I asked the boy.

He laughed too hard, covered his mouth with his fist like he could cough. Where we going? he asked, but I didn't answer. I didn't give him no destination cause then we'd have gotten there. And then what.

He turned us down a dirt road, parked us alongside some trees. Well, he said.

Well, I told him, come here, and the boy did, pulling himself across the bench seat and me under him, the door handle at my neck and that was good, I like to remember it ain't always ideal, and the boy kissed me, his tongue fluttering in my mouth like it was a wounded butterfly, I realized this was his technique and I was touched at the effort.

You need to tell me something, tell me anything, the boy said, holding himself up, he was breathing hard, I thought of his girl, how she gave me some gold hoops for my birthday, how they turned my ears green but I never said, how she snorted when she really got going.

I can't sing, I told the boy. And I ain't no bitch like your brother called me. The boy lowered himself back down upon me, that weight and that heat making me feel all exploded, I was like to breathe him all up and in, Yes you are, he said, I could feel his breath on my face, yes you are a bitch, I could see up close how he was freckled, he smelled like grass and dirt, his heart like a mallet, ain't you, he said, ain't you?

YOU AND YOUR CATS

You got the cat you came to know as Milton the day that Indonesian man phoned up to say he wouldn't be meeting you at the Sizzle Steak because your new hairdo reminded him of a hive of blood beetles, which was a bad omen, and while he was at it your perfume reminded him of his momma's deathbed breath, and finally he spluttered how you make him sad, and that was really the thing of it, this put you off so much you didn't deign to ask him what a blood beetle was, even though that was the best part of the Indonesian man, the exotic facts he could drop into a conversation, like that time he mentioned in passing that he boiled his shoes every week, and was a blood beetle an annoyance similar to the house roach or was it a horror similar to a flying ant, you don't know and now you never will, you daubed some hand soap on your pulse points so you wouldn't smell like breath no more and you went to the Pets 'n' Friends and walked straight to the kitten bucket and pointed, a little boy said, Uhl, that thing got a noface, and you told the boy, Better than too much face, biglips, and you named that cat Milton and you tried not to look directly into its face, cause you remembered the Indonesian man saying how cats can hypnotize you into digging out your own internal organs and offering them up as an afternoon snack.

Then you got Posy cause Milton had gone, you came home one day and he was nowhere, and he was nowhere the next day, and you didn't waste much time after that cause you found yourself thinking of the Indonesian man, how his mouth was just a line, how his eyes were the color of moss, how his jacket smelled like an old onion, which you now realize was likely his body odor and not some secret passion for cooking he would reveal after you had taken him into your bed, which you imagine happening after he had fought off a rapist he found in the alley, but you don't have an alley, and you ain't got Milton either, and you got tired of standing in the fridge light to sniff an old dried onion from the salad drawer, and so there you was at Pets 'n' Friends, pointing again, this one you named Posy cause of her little bud nose, and let's face it cause she had a prominent pink butthole, which she seemed proud of or at least comfortable with, in a way that made you start thinking maybe your hive-head and breathneck weren't ugly things, they just were, and maybe you was all right in the long run, you had nice fingernails after all, and sometimes when you was tired your eyes didn't boggle quite so much, and Posy loved life the way you wish you did, you caught her sitting in the sink so she could watch her own face in the mirror, and she was always rubbing her sides on things, like contact with the drywall was a pleasure sweet enough to be repeated daily, you tried it once but there was nothing there for you.

Then one day Milton was back, flopped in the kitchen watching Posy lick her private details, and you had the feeling you had just walked in during the pillow talk portion of procreation, and you was probably right cause Posy birthed a litter a couple months later, had em right underneath your dining table, left a stain the color of the fancy drink you had on your first dinner with the Indonesian man, Pink Sunrise is what it was called, Posy basking in her spill and Milton somewhere else, what did he care really, four kittens lived and one came out balled tight and not breathing, and you buried it in the backyard, and you cried cause you figured someone had to mourn the loss.

So now you had Milton Posy Pink Sunrise Squints and FluffFluff. And one day you saw the Indonesian man drive by your house in his white four-door, very slow, the sun running a flashing diamond from the hood to the trunk as he passed, you couldn't see his face but his hair looked big, looked womanish, you did not let that stop you from believing it was him, you needed it to be him, and that night you finally relented and welcomed the two stray cats you had been feeding inside, Posy clawed the one but that seemed to be the end of the matter, now you had eight, and you were nine. You had been watching from the window every day and part of the night. The Indonesian man had driven by, it was a fact that snapped into place with a satisfying click, you pulled it out, no it wasn't him, you placed it again, click, it was him, you clicked and clicked and clicked.

Your two strays whelped litters of their own, you noticed how kittens in both had bits of gray the way Milton had bits of gray, you wanted to feel something about it but you couldn't drum nothing up. Now you had fifteen. You didn't see the point of naming them. You had the thought maybe they should name you. Wisp, Haunt, Treatfingers.

You couldn't keep up with the litter box, and one wasn't enough, or two or three, so you sprinkled litter over the linoleum in the downstairs bathroom, you sprinkled till there were dunes, and you felt satisfied at the solution. You left the back door open day and night, you put flypaper up and it worked okay, you saw that another stray had come to stay, and then another, but them cans of Fancy Feast weren't all that much to begin with, so you started buying in bulk. At night you slept faceup in your bed. You could see the fan blades going round and round, you could see the headlights sweeping into your room as a car passed and then sweeping right out again. Something about these cars passing compelled you to do something. Life was out there. Do what? Your stomach was a hot stone. Your heart raced. But you did nothing, what could you do? You had decided if it was the man driving by it was best he didn't see you watching for him. You watched the fan, the cats moaned, you fell asleep, you woke up. You fell asleep.

One day the phone rang. The Indonesian man? No. A neighbor. The cats gathered in the yard at night and made a racket, it was too much, did you understand? You placed the phone in its cradle. The gall of your neighbor, not being the Indonesian man. Your cats wove in and out of your legs. You felt braided, your insides most of all, tightly wound and fastened snug. You dumped can after can of Fancy Feast, some of it splat on their heads. You ran a finger through a blob of tuna 'n veggies between a white one's ears, licked your finger clean. You did that until the white one's head was blobfree, you opened a new can and picked at it with a fork until you were full.

And then one day a woman came to your door while you were grooming your forearms. The woman looked official, her pelvis threatened to burst out her khakis, she had a badge of some kind, a man in sunglasses waited for her on the driveway. Is it the Indonesian man? you asked. The woman stared into your house with her mouth open. Your cats wove and wove. The man, you repeated. Has something happened to the man? Your eyes stung, your cats moaned, it sounded like one long No. The man in the driveway jogged over and looked in. They were from Animal Control, you saw that now. You looked down at your feet, where a turd had appeared, curled over your big toe. The Indonesian man had once told you a story about how, fishing as a boy, he'd reeled in a diaper, how his father had made him pose for a picture with his catch. You remembered how the Indonesian man had pushed your hand when you'd reached for his elbow.

The man in the sunglasses gagged, wondered in a whiny voice why lonely cat ladies were his problem. You wanted to hug him for saying so, for thinking it was loneliness made you what you was. Lonely was normal. Come in but mind the dunes, you told your visitors.

RV PEOPLE

We're in the RV. Someone coughs like a baby's rattle. One of us left the last time we stopped for gas. We were in the aisles of the convenience store looking for sausages, air fresheners, some kind of prophylactic. We are the type to look for things. Then one of us was gone, we saw him walking slowly toward the highway, and some of us watched while he turned against the flow of traffic, and some of us watched when he got into another car, and some of us watched the glint on the windows of that car, light flashing on the windows like some kind of magic trick, and we turned back to our aisles, we turned back to the rest of us, and we paid for the gas and lifted some candies and passed them around us when we were back in the RV. A few of us looked around and asked after the one that left, for them it was like poof, he was gone, did he have ash blond hair, did he prefer to drive in the afternoons? No one answered and we were back on the road anyway.

Later one of us mentions the heat, we're in the desert now, we don't remember how or why we headed in that direction, we breathe the dry heat in and try to remember to let it back out. A few of us work tying knots in a rope, tying a cat's paw, then a clove hitch, then a half blood. Tying, untying. Someone ties a noose and we look away for a while, we can feel her eyes on us but we don't look, she needs to learn. We hit a bump and stop, back up, hit the bump again. Someone in the front says, Had to make sure it was dead, and we sit while some of us are out there cutting it up, discarding what we don't want, making neat cuts we can all agree on. When we get going again the meat is stowed in the cooler, we are running low on ice and we worry about the keep, some of us worrying the blood on our fingers, using our mouths before it can dry, but it's hard to get under the nails just right.

We drive all the night, keeping each other company. We say things about the abundance of stars, so much light, but we don't really care for stars, there are other things to notice, like woodgrain, like a sheet on the line, like the tender parts of the naked among us, like the smell of anything after it's cut into. Some of us shuffle cards, deal them out, we make piles of cards, they are worn like dollars now, a two of clubs gives out, crumbles in our laps, we push the bits onto the floor, some of us collect the bits later on.

At an all-night diner we pick up more of us, some of us are convincing enough to get a waitress to leave her pad and apron behind, some of us are lonely enough to take a woman and her baby. The woman cries all night long, even when we make soothing noises, even when we hand her our treasures: two river stones, silver foil, a braid of hair. We take her baby from her, we pass it forward, we rock it in our arms.

Close to dawn we drive off the road, into the desert. We park and arrange ourselves to sleep. Some of us are on the dining bench. Some of us lie on the floor, stomach to back, half to half, so there is enough room. Some of us take the bed in the back, touch each other in the agreed-upon way. Some of us cry out and are ashamed. We close our eyes. We open them hours later. Two have left, we see their footprints in the sand outside, heading farther into the desert. We follow the footprints for a time. We turn when we are in danger of losing sight of the RV. We think it was two men, we count ourselves, we think it was a man and his boy, they have left their bar of soap, they took a few cuts of meat, there are drippings down the narrow walkway and down the steps. Some of us get behind the RV and push it back to the road, digging our toes in, most of us are barefoot, some of us are prideful of the thick soles of our feet, but that pride is frowned upon.

We drive. Some of us are sick into the bucket. Some of us check for ingredients, flavorings, there are none. There is only the cooler. The waitress passes white packets of sugar from her pocket, some of us feed from the new woman's breast, but it is work. We barter for clothing, for secrets, for touch. We wear what we find. We claim what we can. We say *sss sss sss* into our ears. We say hush, hush. Some of us lean into each other and touch. We are bored. We don't say this but it is what we are. Some of us put mouths to mouths, use our teeth, some of us try not to mind.

In the evening there is a red sky. We notice how it bleeds into the horizon instead of out. A few of us pass the drippings cup, but soon there's none left.

In the morning one of us kills another of us. We are not sure how, there is no blood. There is torn clothing, a broken cup. Some of us try to mourn, some of us sing over the body, we lay the rope in a thief's knot over the heart. We think how sad that what made your life something woulda happened whether you existed or didn't. We forget who of us did the killing, it don't matter.

On another day we wake and we are fewer. On this day we remember who is missing: the waitress, the momma, her baby. We remember because they are new, and it is an abomination to shed the new. More footsteps leading out, into the desert, away. We feel skinned. They are new, and they have gone. We look among us, we all agree. We gather things: throwing things, catching things, stabbing things. Rope, always rope. We tie the rope to the RV, we press our feet into the footprints of the escaped, we keep hold of the rope. We have lost some of us, but we will not be lost.

It is not long before the footprints become draggings, we can see them ahead, how they struggle to go on. Some of us exalt, speak our language. Some of us use our weapons on ourselves, we are so eager. We are the type to look for things, we are saying. Up ahead they are slowing. We begin to run.

CLOCKS

Momma says Jean's just a imaginary friend, but I tell Jean Momma's just a imaginary bitch.

Jean's a yarnhead.

Jean says that ain't nice to repeat but it's true, it's what she is, and based on the pictures she draw it is clear her momma is a yarnhead also.

You gotta be careful around the scissors cause yarn don't grow back. That's how come Jean's so sensitive.

Jean told me once she saw my daddy wipe his stuff with a kitchen towel.

I have to leave Jean at home when I go off to school cause otherwise the kids will be jealous about how I got a stuck clock where my brain's supposed to be, that's how my momma explained it and it makes sense.

The clock by my daddy's side of the bed ain't stuck, but it ain't telling the time either. Noon. Midnight. Noon.

Jean tells me if I spend time fixing on details like that I'll drive myself to drink. This our new best thing to say.

We like anything where a key is needed. Keep that secret locked up tight now, girlie.

That's our second-best thing to say.

Me and Jean play like we spies sometimes, we used a old flashlight for a while, but in the daylight you don't need no more light and in the nighttime we got too scared, you should only spy if you really want to find something.

And we didn't really want to all that much.

Noon's okay. Midnight, though.

If you take off Jean's clothes there ain't nothing really to see. White cloth, black thread. No bumps or creases. I pray for Jean's body but I wasn't born a yarnhead and that's the cross I have to bear.

Jean and me been studying my face in the mirror, looking hard at it, and we pretty sure it's still my face. And that is a relief.

Jean says it's all right to grow up and get old and die without ever taking a man for your own. That's another relief.

Jean says there's no need to set your hair or wear red nails or spritz lilac stuff behind your ears, if somebody don't want that kind of attention then that is A-OK.

I see my momma do all these things, but it don't seem to matter. I don't do none of them, but that don't seem to matter either.

Jean says my daddy been throwing some of my stuff in the trash. She's right, I know some of my stuff is gone, but I don't fix on the details.

At school a boy named Bo asks me do I want to meet him behind the swings, there's a brick wall we can duck down behind, I say sure cause that seems the easiest.

Recess at noon. Or midnight? One is 12, the other is 12, so ain't they the same? All of it's the same, what Bo got to show and what I seen at the other 12, I'd like to talk it over with Jean but like I said she ain't allowed to school, I tell Bo about the two 12s but he ain't listening, I saw Bo had one of them fungus nails on his pinky finger, thick and green, the button on his pants shiny as a new penny, the bell rang and I went into the little girls' and up-chucked the egg my momma fried me that morning.

At lunch I traded my sandwich for a pink pencil, cause Jean loves pencils and we never seen a pink one.

Jean says, Did you feel better? I say I did.

Jean says to hide, and we do, and we whisper how any minute we could pee, and I want to laugh and yawn all at once cause I feel so happy to be with Jean, but we have to keep quiet cause we're hiding, and the first one to make a noise during loses.

We never talk about what happens if you win at hiding.

Hiding always ends with Daddy finding us.

Daddy asks me do I want to ride on his motorcycle and I say yes even though Jean says I'm a dumb bitch.

Just around the block a few times, my daddy says, and then I need you to help me out with something in the garage. I don't listen to that last part. I go stuck clock. My face ain't my face. I think how we'll ride past that mailbox with the wood ducks and that flat dead cat in the road, and that house that got burned up by a drug addict. Wind in my hair, my hair that ain't yarn.

Jean don't have a daddy, so she don't know. Cause how can you tell your own daddy no? You can't. If you can I'm sorry for you.

A GIRL

There was a girl gone missing a few years back. Her momma standing out front of the Dairy Queen, eyeing your cone like you was hiding her child within. You seen Dee? Dee Switcher? You seen her? Nope was always the answer, but I'll keep an eye out. And before you knew it that cone was gone.

That was the year that old bitch Miss Shane was teaching us algebra. Solve for *x*, children. Chalk dusting her dress like she had a ghost dress on over her other one. Them arms like dough on a spit.

That missing girl used to do her eyeliner during class. Over and over, underlining her eye like Miss Shane underlined them nasty equations. Solve for *x*.

We all had plans for that girl. She had a chest. She smoked them long thin lady cigarettes in plain sight of the custodian. When that retarded boy ran into the girl and knocked her purse down a condom spilled out, flashing there in its gold wrapper, looking for all the world like a coin.

The girl picked up her lipsticks and wallet and hair things and left it there, left that condom on the ground and walked off. Us thinking hard about ways to spend that coin.

There was other girls of course. The entire cheerleading team could get you going, save for the chubby one, but she'd do in a pinch. The majorette, Glenda was her name, rumor had it she'd drink too much at parties and beg you to fondle her.

So it wasn't like this girl was the cream of the crop or nothing, there was plenty of girls. We wanted them all, Dee Switcher included.

Her momma was the town skank. Everybody knew. So you couldn't take her all that seriously when her girl went missing. Stay home all night for once, our own mommas would whisper to each other, swat each other on the arm. You so bad. I know it.

Nobody ever picked up that condom. It got kicked around and pushed into corners, and once Dee went missing we all got scared of it, and kicked it harder. Girls would shriek should they see it rocketing toward them. Some boys too.

Then one day we all realized it wasn't there no more. Probably the custodian got it. Or it was somewhere no one cared to look.

Her daddy came to the school on a Monday morning, no one had seen her daddy in years, but here he was asking where was Dee, why did the school let her skip so easy, where was the truant officer, demanding to know who took her, who had his girl? We watched the principal pet his shoulder like you would a sick animal, watched Dee's daddy get led to the door, it was a bright day and for a second he got swallowed up by the glare. He didn't come back.

There was a big homecoming dance a few months after the girl went gone. We all paired up and parted our hair and wore suit coats and danced slow when we were told to.

Dee's momma showed up at the dance in a fancy night-gown thing, asking could she chaperone. We watched the principal lead her over to the punch bowl, but Dee's momma wasn't there for long, no one came for punch and after a few songs she walked out with her head so high you worried for her neck.

Some of us met at the diner after, eating pancakes while our girls fiddled with our belt loops under the table, if you were lucky. Others of us went to the after party at the Days Inn, but that turned out to be a bust. The stereo ran out of batteries and Miss Shane's son showed up and puked into the trash can and everybody went home.

Dee had left school after fifth period, was the story. Snuck out while everyone was scrambling for their lockers. Rumor had it she was going with an older boy, he might could even be called a man. One day a skinny lady cop came and asked a few of us what we knew, but really we didn't know nothing.

We skipped school all the time, was the thing. Sometimes it felt like if you didn't skip you'd close your eyes and die, right there in the middle of Civics, so you did skip, and you'd go to the Circle K to buy Slim Jims or over to a friend's house to look at his dad's titty magazines. And nothing bad ever happened.

The lady cop seemed to find us not knowing nothing a relief. That's what I figured, she'd say in agreement with you. Which meant, to us, solving for *x* really was an impossibility, a waste of time, so why bother?

At Christmastime Miss Shane told us she had skin cancer, she wouldn't be back the next semester. We stared at that mole on her cheek, as we had done for months. That's what I figured, some of us wanted to blurt. Miss Shane's eyes went wet, we started feeling soft toward her, but after she assigned two chapters of homework for over the break we went back to hating her guts, which felt better, more normal, than feeling sorry for her, so in a way you got to feeling grateful toward her for being such a cooze.

Over the break we saw Dee's little brother at the movies by hisself. We forgot all about him, but there he was with his money in a wad, staring up at the listings like he couldn't read. We went on in and spent all our money on arcade games. Then later that night, in your bed that smelled like socks and sweat and secretions and powder Tide, if you weren't careful you'd start thinking how when you came out the boy was gone, and how maybe you should feel regretful about not inviting him to man the firetorch gun, really the best gun to have if you were playing Immortal Fear and you made it past the first two rounds, which everyone did.

But he had gone.

That winter someone found the girl's yellow purse on the side of the road. The strap was gone. One of us heard their dad saying how you could use a strap to strangle someone, or at least tie up her hands. Her perfume bottle was smashed. That girl ain't coming back, we told each other, shifting our nuts like we'd seen our dads do whenever they said something serious.

But really, we already knew that. You just had to say some things out loud.

During the spring semester Miss Shane's boy got in a fistfight with the custodian. No one knew why but we figured it was stressful, having a bitch mom who had cancer. Then on Palm Sunday a dog found a skull and carried it to his master's doorstep. There was excitement for a time, but it turned out to be the skull of an infant, probably buried by some of them country folk who can't afford no funeral.

A rumor got spread that a girl tasted like a 9-volt battery down there. It got hot, hotter than the last summer, and a old lady died in her house cause she was too weak to open some windows.

We'd see Dee's momma working as the greeter at the Walmart. If she recognized you she'd say, Seen Dee? Dee Switcher? and most of the time we just shook our head, stared at our shoes till we got to the magazines aisle. Guns and girls, we needed more info on both.

Some of us got for-real girlfriends. Some of us snuck into their rooms at night and made love, you had to call it making love or your girl got mad, to these girls while you listened to their dads sawing logs just to the other side of the wall, you biting your girl's pillow hard so you wouldn't make no noise, you ignoring how sometimes your girl just laid there, her fingertips on your back limp and uninterested, you despite the dud your girl turned out to be feeling like your bottom half was exploding up into your top.

Dee one time punched a girl in the mouth, she'd been crying hard just before, her face ruined, black smears down her cheeks and her upper lip all glistened with snot. By that time we knew girls sometimes got ugly. Dee got sent home, came back the next day with her makeup all set again. Lips all wet. Eyes so blue you got to feeling indecent. See, we had seen Dee, we'd seen her a lot, but back then we had our eyes on all the girls, and over time it got to be hard to see how losing one was such a tragedy.

HEART

The man griddling pancakes don't look me in the eyes when he fills my plate. His eyes drift upward toward my hairline, skitter down to my neck, I feel for the man, I ain't easy to look at.

I feel for the man, that's one hallway, but down another hallway I watch myself beat the man with my tray until his head's a broken gurgling pie.

My momma always said I got a head shaped like a heart. Not like them cartoon hearts bitch girls draw about other boys in their notebooks. Like the real thing. A pumping chambered ugly of a muscle not meant for no light of day. Guess that means instead of brains I'm all blood. Guess that's why I ain't ever been scared of blood.

It's warm like I'm warm. It pools thick and gorgeous and don't step in it less you want to make a painting of what you done for any passing bitch to start hollering about.

Rest of me's just flesh. Mounds and folds of flesh, rubbing against itself, slick like a tongue through a mouth. When I feel rotten I pretend all that sweat is blood, my insides pouring out, the sky above me narrowing to a speck till there ain't no sky and there ain't no me.

But then I always wake up, my head and heart pounding, clobbering me all to shit.

I ask the pancakes man does he know if there's pie, he points his spatula away from himself, I turn in that direction but he is pointing at the soda machine. I feel that spider I get in my belly again, that prickly thing. I close my eyes, push the corner of my tray into my belly till it hurts and past till it hurts, till the pain feels normal and that spider's a goner.

It ain't the man's fault, the spider, I got to keep reminding myself it ain't people's fault.

A lady in scrubs rings me up. Tonight it's pancakes, a waffle, curls of bacon, a dish of macaroni and Velveeta, a good-size fluff of scrambled eggs, a wrapped sandwich for later, a salad I ain't going to eat. A wedge of cake, red with white frosting. The lady's flesh is the color of honey, flecked with tiny dark freckles. I wonder is something wrong with her, that honey color and everything, then I realize I like it, I like that color, I like this lady in her shirt of colored cats. I say, You like pussycats, huh? But the lady says, No, like I just asked her did she like eating babies, holds out her hand for the money.

Another thing about me is, I got a real hard time showing my true emotions. So inside me there is a roaring, I am the roaring, it shreds the lady before me, it hangs her by her cat shirt, her tongue pink as a lozenge, but outside me I thank the lady, ask her could she just keep the change.

I sit way in the back of the lunching room. There's only a few other people here, a crying lady crumpled over her tea, two thugs in white uniforms, holding them plastic spork things in their skinny fists, a man watching a little girl fingering dimples into her mashed potatoes.

Momma and I at Wekiva Springs. Me eating a Dole Whip, licking it off my forearm, my elbow, mistaking salt for sugar. The man Momma was with slapping the cone from my hand, That's enough, Fatty, he said, Momma laughing, Momma telling me to go off by myself for a while. The water lapping quietly, the light in the trees. Momma sprinkling Ajax over my ice cream. *That's so you won't have a taste for it no more.* Momma serving dirt from the yard over milk. *You eat that, you can have dessert.* I ate it.

I'd still eat it. But I don't want no one watching me.

From the back of the room I can see out the windows, the sun finally gone, a jagged pink-orange stripe all that's left of the day, like someone melted a taffy and made a nasty smear. My mouth is watering, I want to jam all that food in my mouth at once, even my napkin, even my straw and cup and utensils and packet of salt, I want to go over and eat the mashed potatoes off the girl's plate, suck the bits off her fingers, try not to bite down.

I wonder does anyone else ever feel this way. Does anyone else ever feel like the wrapper to the taffy.

When I'm done I use the pads of my fingers to get the crumbs, I don't want to leave nothing behind. *Graso*, one of the thugs says, sniggers into his hand.

Blood in my heart, blood in my head. It's a comfort sometimes to think about all the waves of blood lapping just under the surface, all around me.

The thugs get up, still laughing. Down one hallway, I laugh along, down another, I

SPLITS

Momma says you can't get pregnant if you do the splits and hold your breath for one whole minute after the boy makes his deposit, she watches TV like that, toes pointed, chest tight, sometimes her cheeks puff out like a blowfish I guess, I never seen a blowfish.

Momma's got friends, David, Joey, Lar, the man with the ears, the man with the briefcase, Jed, the man with the teeth. Sometimes they stay for dinner.

Most nights I push my bike up the hill so I can ride it back down. All us kids used to do it in the neighborhood but I'm the only one still does. I'm not sure what the other kids do now.

I don't like riding down the hill. Toward the end I go so fast that I'm sure I'll crash. But it's what I do in the evenings.

At school a boy pushes his finger into the flesh at my belly and says, You have a fat stomach. We are in science class, he has made a scientific discovery, another boy tries with his finger but I kick him in his checkbook.

I am suspended, I walk home. There is a car in front of our house so I keep walking. It's hot, air like the inside of a mouth. I walk to the grocery store, read some greeting cards, there is one in the humorous row that I can't understand. At the deli counter I order a bag of sliced turkey. I eat what I can in the bathroom, flush what I don't finish.

On the walk back I suddenly get it. Sweat falling like tears. The sun white and singing. Dumb card, dumb everything.

The car is gone, Momma is in the kitchen holding a bag of peas to her arm. Battle scars, she says, winking. She lowers slowly, toes squeaking on the tile, she is in her underwear and I can see her pubic hair. She holds her breath, I take the peas from her to refreeze.

While we're watching our Tuesday program the doorbell rings, Momma looks surprised, brushing at her sweatpants, it's clear she isn't expecting no friends tonight. I let the man in while she freshens up, Momma calls out, Sit tight, the bed ain't made or nothing, the man asks me about school but he's looking at the TV.

Pushing my bike up the hill I can't help it, I look in other people's windows, some are watching the same program me and Momma were, some are just sitting around a table. I imagine being a stranger walking by and looking in Momma's window right now, seeing the empty kitchen, the TV on but no one watching, crumpled dress pants outside the door to the back bedroom.

At the top of the hill I see a group of them, sitting on a car under the streetlamp and smoking. Hey, fatgut, one of them calls. A girl in a pink skirt laughs, I recognize her as the girl who got her period all over her gym shorts, she had to go to the school nurse and get a pair of pants from the lost and found. In elementary school I'd spent the night at her house once, we messed with her momma's makeup and jewelry and she got slapped. Yeah, fatgut, she says.

Through our window you can see a picture of me on the wall, the only picture we have up. It's from when I was a kid. That's what I'd want to look at, walking by our house and looking in, thinking, Who is that, where is she?

I still haven't gotten my period, sixteen years old and no period, Momma says I'm lucky, no splits for me yet. I don't tell Momma there'd be no need for splits anyway.

I don't wait for them to say something else, I park my bike and lift my shirt so they can see it, pale under the streetlamp. This what I look like, I tell them. This who I am, you don't got to tell me. The air is sharp on my skin. They look. They look and look.

If I had the guts I'd tell Momma she's dumb for believing something like that. For thinking I don't hear her in there with her friends, wailing like something run over. If I had a different kind of guts, I mean.

SUMMER MASSACRE

Picnic with the in-laws, Gavin's grandparents. Jim watched Em's mom bring over a tray. Fizzing glasses, grapes, butterscotches. When Jim had first met Em's mom, she had an edge to her. That tray would have been all salt. Now it was all sweet and shine and fizz, butterscotches on every plate. Don't you just love that noise? She meant the wrapper, that throatless whine, the yolk freed from its shell. Ah! Em's mom placing it on her tongue, her cheek always pouched these days. Em's hand on Jim's knee. Gavin braiding dandelions to wreathe around the dog. Em's dad behind his chair, swishing his ice. Why's he doing that? Why're you doing that, kid? Because Mitzi is a princess, said Gavin. Em's dad cutting his eyes at Jim, the lenses in his bifocals yellowed to butterscotch. Goodbye, drink. You bring your glove? What glove? Jesus. Dad, Em warned. Em's mom torturing another wrapper. Nin, it seemed to be saying, nin! The dog licked Jim's ankle, its tongue rapturous, slow, really savoring it. Jim closed his eyes. A butterscotch behind each eyelid, flamed in red. A bloody yolk, the sun exploding. If the end of the world came . . . what? If the end of the world came . . . but he just felt tired. If the end of the world came, good night.

•••

Sundrops, dollops of sun, your own collection of sunshine! In a bowl. If the bowl was a universe it'd be filled with suns. If I was a universe I'd be a universe that swallowed that bowl universe. My blood is a sunbeam. Who used to call them sundrops? My mother. Her mother? A mother of some sort. Emily is a mother, right? Right? There is her son, Gavin. Brock likes to call him Gayvin when we're alone. Brock's little mouth, that chute of ash. He's volcanic! I spill sunbeams, I can't help it. Ah, the rapture. I mean the wrapper! Its halfhearted struggle, its little voice. Like the squeak of an infant. Emily, blam! Shot out like I was the volcano. The doctor nearly dropped her. Should've used a net! Everyone laughed. Brock's white white face. Me, an emptied bowl. Oh, Jim's asleep. That wide wet mouth. That rubbery ring above his belt. I've imagined him and my daughter, what mother hasn't? Brock always says, Soft in the stomach, soft in the heart.

But I've seen him with Mitzi. Knuckles massaging her ears, little bits of hot dog to snuffle out of his palm. You're a good girl, aren't you? But was he asking Mitzi, or was he asking me? It's simple: if you've already got one in your mouth, use the other cheek.

•••

Mom. Mm? Emily's knuckle gathering up the yellowed glistening pocket at the corner of her mother's mouth. A little sunshine for you, sweets. Yes, thank you. And smeared it onto her skirt. When Gavin was a baby she'd often wonder if her clothes were held together with his saliva. Her shoulder a collection of glistening webs. Drying into armor. Look at him now, a person like she was a person. Songs with violins made her sad, she'd once climbed out her window to make love to a boy under her father's beloved willow tree, the smell of onions always reminded her of the summer she nearly drowned. What were Gavin's violins, his willow, his onions? But that could never be known. She hadn't even told Jim about the willow, and what was the point of mentioning the onions? The meaning was hers and hers only. Last month Gavin had kissed the neighbor's boy, a lunging violent stab of a kiss she saw from the kitchen window. The neighbor's boy had backed away, still holding the toy shovel they'd been using to bury a Ziploc of treasures. Wiping his mouth over and over. The shovel sailing through the air, Gavin catching it, the neighbor boy turning to run. Gavin at eleven. At forty he might come upon his own son's toy shovel . . . and what? She tried to remember his face as the boy backed away. Fear? Shame? Triumph? She could only think how she had felt, climbing back into her bedroom, trailing bits of grass, crumbs of dirt, as she came toward her mirror. Who is that? Me. Yes, but who?

•••

Banner day! You hear yourself saying those words, you had been thinking those words because that's what Pop used to say on days like these, the sky blue as a swimming pool and the sun all light and no heat and the smell of barbecue coming from three yards over. But really everything hurts your eyes, the ice in your glass, your wife's precious butterscotches, the color of your son-in-law's shirt, the face of your grandson's delicate wristwatch, even the shine of your daughter's hair. You had been trying to sound cheerful. But you heard yourself. Banner day, ploop ploop, two turds. So be it. Your knee goes zing when you lean over to nudge Mitzi off your son-in-law's ankle. The boy gasps, thinks you kicked her. Let him. Toughen him up. As a boy you were teased mercilessly. Big ears, thin legs, patched shirts, you were once chased into the woods and punched so hard you felt bits of your nose stream down your throat. Zing, the knee again. Pop had said, My poor son, you poor thing. You hadn't hit back, not once. Fell to the ground, your hands over your face, watched the light in the leaves through your fingers. The boys were quiet about it. A serious business. Like butchers tenderizing a cut of meat. Pop had gently cleaned your face with one of your mother's good washcloths and lavender soap until you felt sorry for yourself. Even now, you hate him for that.

•••

The boy is thinking, Dandelions don't really smell. Neither do daisies. I mean I guess they smell like dirt and grass. Mitzi smells like stale cake. Mom smells like oranges. Dad smells like nothing. If you scratch hard enough and then smell your fingers, you'll smell whatever part of your body you just scratched. The boy's body smells like lots of things. Buttered popcorn, the vinegar his mother uses to wash the floors, tomato sauce. The boy reminds himself, Smells are important in case you go blind. Dad says when the end of the world comes you don't know what can happen. Your eyes might get burned out of your head. Mitzi's digging, that smells like dirt of course. And dirt smells like dirt. The boy's favorite smells are smells that don't smell like anything else. Mitzi's wreath has already fallen off. I'll leave it, he thinks. If I try to put it back on, Grandpop might ask me about the glove again. The boy has already discovered that sometimes people decide things about you and you just have to let them. The boy plans on one day being a talk show guest. The host will blindfold him, hold Styrofoam cups in front of his nose. Worms, the boy will say. Cream of Wheat. Root beer. Paste. My balls. That'll be his joke when the cup is filled with tomato sauce. That's incredible! the host will say, pumping the boy's hand. Applause. Starburst camera flashes from the darkness. The boy has read that space smells like cinnamon. He can't imagine why. But better to think about that, and wonder if the sun really smells like a melted crayon like he thinks or like butterscotch like Grandmom says. Better that than kissing, better that than being called a fag at the bus stop. A million melted crayons worth of better.

•••

Mitzi dug under the willow tree. Den of bunnies, she knew it! Flung one by one into the sun. What the? the old man said. His glass landed too hard on the table, glass on glass, the sound of a bright bright ending. Is it over? the younger man lurching awake. She's killing them! this from the boy. Don't look! from the younger woman. Oh, Brock, the old woman tried to say. Her mouth lined with candies. The bunnies gritted with dirt, the satisfying crunch! Little mewling whines, nin! Nin! All out now. Writhing ones first, pink as antacids. Gray one, still as a stone in the grass. Yolks tumbling from the old woman's mouth, Brock! The old man with his hands to his face. The younger woman, flap of skirt, yanking hand. Rubies of blood on the dog's snout, taffy-tears of pink skin dotting her tongue. The younger man, I was asleep! The bunnies in the grass, unearthed and scattered, twitching, all but the gray one. The old man, No, oh no. The dog a grin. The younger woman bent over the dog. The old woman, lapful of sunbeams, They're suffering! The old man to his knees despite his knee. And the boy. The boy thinking, Cinnamon, cinnamon. The boy walking slow, the boy raising his leg and bringing it down firm as a hammer onto the pinks, one by one, each one a starburst under his shoe, all quiet now, all dark, he knew what was in this cup, but he'd never be able to say.

LIKE

We are at, like, a dance. We are like wearing these new tops. We put lipstick all around our mouths. We feel jealous of each other's mouth, but like that isn't cool so we keep it to ourselves. We don't want to dance with anything chubby because it's like dancing with our stepdads, or dancing with some like weird baby grizzly boy. We are like yuck. We want to dance with anything that plays football or like golf. Anything that like might play the savior in a movie or a TV show. Or like the killer. We wouldn't mind being, like, bladed. We some of us don't have titties but some of us do and it is hard to be, like, happy about it. The other day we felt each other's chests in the locker room. Like some of us got called ant bite and some of us got called pudding piles. Some of us agreed that, like, pudding piles are just fat, just floppy mounds of gross fat and it's like do some push-ups. But then later we all were thinking how it'd be okay to have some fat because then your like top would look better and like maybe the quarterback would ask you to get in his car. Some of us felt more than each other's chest in the locker room but, like, whatever, it's the locker room. Some of us get all burned up in the locker room. We like, like, watching. Like thinking about being in some guy's car could happen at any time and, like, a lot of the time it happens in the locker room. Some of us have, like, been in that car. Some of us like have, like, bite marks and we love how they're like rainbows, purple green yellow gone. Some of us bite ourselves because, like, whatever. At this dance we pretend there are arrows pointing out each ant bite or pudding pile right at, like, the savory boys. This helps with our posture and also it's like, You, come. We're, like, always imagining what like the best night would be and it's like someone took a poker and stirred up our embers and, like, whoosh, we're all of us like our own flame. It's like, You, come, and bring that poker. We can like taste it. Some of us are thinking bratwurst, like how our stepdads cook sometimes, all cooked and, like, firm and ready to be eaten. And, like, the juices. Some of us know better because we've been in that car. Like there's no platter, there's no, like, small bites. There's no stopping when you get full. We're at this dance and some of us keep going to the bathroom to sip out of this bottle of, like, iced tea but like it's only half iced tea and like the other half is rum. We throw our heads back to get it down. Our throats are jagged and it's, like, who needs a poker? We take our shoes off and slouch in the bathroom and it's like what a relief and like we all see each other the way we are in the locker room and it's like we're just girls and like we hate each other for our hair and legs and titties and mouths and even like wrists, but we would never say that to each other because that's not how you like treat a friend. And we'll be friends forever so like we hate each other until our hate turns into like love. Some of us have dreams that we're carrying the others of us on our shoulders because the others of us are like dead, and *foom* we drop the bodies into this big like fire and there goes the hair there goes the eyelashes there goes the like perfect Disney princess wrists, but the others of us probably have the same dream because like they want to watch our ankles and tans and thighs burn until we're just meat, so it's like we get each other. We put our shoes back on and point the arrows out again and like we're back in the gym waiting and we get pulled onto the dance floor and we like put our hands on our boys' necks and like some of us swirl our nails in our boys' hair and some of us are rewarded with like little denim or khaki animals, little sea monkeys we make grow with like barely any work on our part. We pretend we don't know our hips are swiveling or, like, some of us are short so we have to really work our abs, and our boys hold us tight and we smell their deodorant and cologne and sweat and like their essence under it all, which is like garlic and like dirt. And our boys probably think they are doing it to us too, like we're, like, buckling and folding and melting, but that is like pretending that the stars in the sky are just the pearl buttons on our tops and skirts, just unfasten and zoom the heat of the universe of our like necks and titties and the parts we spritz and oil the most is our boys' to like have. Like we're like theirs.

But, like, it's us, we lie on our backs to watch the sky pearl to star, we are skin to bite we are hair to flick we are swish, we have the power it's us we say what we want we say, Come, and we say, Here, and we say, Burn, and we say, Like.

THE NOISE

There was that noise again. Definitely something mechanical.

His stomach roiled; he pictured a swordfish wearing a parsley lei stabbing through the slosh of coffee and bourbon and, when the night got late and he felt tired of paying for premium booze, the gin he felt sure had been ladled from a toilet somewhere in the bowels of the hotel.

The hotel had seemed promising. Its neon sign in a modern sort of font. Industrial lettering or some shit. Maxine would know.

But after pulling his wheeled suitcase through a labyrinth of hallways to get to his room, he realized it wasn't anything different from the Ramada at the end of the strip. Just a hotel room. In fact he wondered could he have smelled the drapes so strongly in that Ramada. Bleach. Exhaust. And something sour, something like rags at the bottom of a well.

They were bright yellow. Frazzles of black lines at odd intervals. He imagined in the Ramada the drapes were hunter green with some mallards or paisley, or both. This hotel was really saying something with these drapes, with that chair made out of clear plastic, with that urchin of a beanbag he found in the bathroom. For what? He had rested his feet on it while on the toilet. Had read the free months-old issue of *Playboy.* It had been placed with the soaps, the mouthwash, the shower cap, all arranged on a fan of towels. Had clearly survived a bath of some sort, maybe more than once, and it gave the pages the feel of a rarefied document, something old and of the import to never, ever be thrown out.

That fucking noise! What was it? Had someone left a dog in the next room? Terrified in the dark, shivering, its eyes two black moons, keeping quiet until it became impossible and out burst a cry, a two-note moaning eruption that the dog immediately felt relieved and reterrified by?

Only, the noise was the same, every time. The clock was on the other side of the king bed, and he felt barred by something—exhaustion? fear, maybe?—from rolling over to look at it, to time the intervals in between the noises.

Instead he convinced himself, again, that he was just hearing the elevator. Something to do with the elevator. Focused on the night he'd had. What had he lost, what had he accrued?

At Caesar's he'd started at the quarter slots, and after four neat bourbons had moved on to the five-dollar slots. Had come in with a grand. Left with thirteen hundred. Thought he saw Maxine at the ATM, nearly grabbed her elbow until he remembered: wasn't her. Heart jabbing wildly. He ate swordfish at the buffet. Could taste the lamp it had been heated under. Hunted a scale from behind a molar, left it on his plate, thought better of it, dropped it into his inner pocket. The way it flashed at him: wink, wink. A real treasure.

At New York, New York, he'd ordered a coffee from a cocktail waitress whose face was smooth, unlined, fresh even, but whose gnarled toes and bunion the size of a cherry tomato told a different story. He tipped her a twenty, she ran her hand down his cheek. He waited for a different waitress, ordered a double bourbon. Won a hundred at craps, two at blackjack. Made it outside in time to heave into a trash can, but only the bourbon came up. A girl holding hands with her grandmother watched him, shook her head and grinned like he was putting on a show for her. He wiped his mouth with the back of his hand, tipped an imaginary hat at her. Wink, wink. Realized too late it was the kind of grin that's the preamble to a gory wave of screaming. Pushed his way forward, away, Oops, he said, oops, I didn't know. Every face a spinning wheel.

The noise couldn't be mechanical. It had the essence of sorrow, of regret. He wanted the clock the way a drowning man must want an inner tube. But he'd have to roll, he'd have to show his back to the window, and the noise was making him feel like that was a bad idea. Like a shrieking carpet of horror would reach him if he turned for the clock. Better to stay on his back, where he could see the window and the short hallway that led to the door.

Would Maxine laugh at him? No. She'd be turned off. Call down and ask, she'd hiss, the smell of sleep pouring out of her, her face creased, her hair in her eyes.

Well, the phone was on the desk across the room. So eat shit, Maxine, and God, it felt good to think it.

There it was again. Was it coming more quickly? Now it sounded like a child who'd been hiding too long, shut in a closet waiting for the game to be over. Olly olly oxen free? He felt threaded with exhaustion. He imagined putting up his hands, No thanks, the inner tube bobbing away.

He'd returned to his hotel, had found a bar, watched some fratty types twitch and lunge at the cocktail waitresses from the rim of his double gin. Had made one of the waitresses giggle when he said, You feel yourself having a powerful craving for beef? Was talking about how they all looked made of meat. Felt good that she got it. Realized later human beings are animals and thus made of meat anyway. But realized that while getting an outside-the-pants squeeze job from a different waitress he'd asked to meet him in the elevator, so the shame was eclipsed and set aside. They were all so smart, these girls. Just had to give them an idea in the neighborhood of what you were thinking and they knew just what you were getting at, could give you directions to your own house.

He'd come in his underwear. Better that way, less cleanup for her. He placed bills one by one into her tiny brown hand until she closed it. The elevator stopped at his floor. Had he pushed the button? They both made a move to get off, but she stopped herself, her face a small brown apple, and swept her hand out, like, Here you go! *Gracias*, he said, and she stared at him so blankly he realized she wasn't Hispanic, just really tan. The mirrored doors came together silently. His two selves joined, and then halved.

The noise again. Not like a child really, more like a man whimpering into a toilet, the bowl splattered with his dinner. And there it was again. Not like the man, more like the elevator. It came from the wall across from the bed. No, it came from the hallway. From the room next door. Someone was watching television, or making love, or both.

He'd taken a bath, brought the *Playboy* in with him to finish reading. Splunk, it'd fallen almost immediately in. Seemed destined. There was a particular girl he'd liked, wearing a blazer and high heels and nothing else. Just all, Here's my vagina, no bones about it. A hint of areola, no nipple. But he'd thrown the magazine in the trash, figured this final bath was the end of the road for it. Now he wondered if it was his girl whimpering in there, crying out from her crimped page. It was stupid! Still, he felt sad about it.

And now it came from the side of his bed, the side with the clock. The floor. The swordfish in his belly quaked, the sword lurched up toward his heart. It reminded him of something. He'd had a dream, as a child, that he'd looked over the side of his bed to see a man with flat black eyes lying there, his mouth full of blood, reaching up clawed hands like Help me. Or like Say goodbye. As an adult he'd found out it wasn't a dream, that an Indian from the nearby reservation had wandered into the house after a bar fight, that his father had come in and dragged the Indian out.

He felt that man's hands reaching up now, crabbing slowly over the side of the bed, hidden in the comforter. The man's tongue probing, blinded by blood.

He ran through his room toward the door. Worked the handle like a baby works a ring of keys. Light in the hallway. Someone was watching TV a few rooms down. The sighs of the elevators. Everything would be okay. He lay down on the carpet outside the room. Maybe everything leaves a ghost. Maybe his ghost was still inside the room. Maybe another ghost was at a slot machine. Maybe Maxine's ghost was a whimper in the dark. It was Maxine who'd always loved Vegas. But he didn't have to care about that anymore.

BRENDA'S KID

On her way to work Brenda stopped by her kid's house to help clear the leaves out of the gutter. He shuffled out in gym shorts and a tank, worked his bare toes into the squelch of the lawn, it had been raining, Brenda wore a 7-Eleven bag over her hair to keep out the damp. Well, she said, and her kid's head snapped to, it was clear he knew he was supposed to do something, get something, offer something, but he couldn't figure what. Brenda said, Ladder, in a gentle but questioning voice, and he answered, I know, I was just, but he didn't finish what he was just, and the mean part of Brenda, the oozing eggplant-colored meanness hissed, He wasn't just anything, and get a load of those love handles, beer-drinking monkeytoed lumberdummy that he is, but Brenda swallowed that down and concentrated on how nicely the aloe she'd planted was coming up, it seemed to love its new pot, orange clay pot, ochre, the word ochre, ochre ochre ochre. Her kid dragged the ladder over, stared at Brenda with his eyebrows raised, like, What now, lady? Brenda let him hold her purse, he slung it up and over his shoulder and stood with his arms folded over his stomach. Don't fall now, he said. The boy had enormous brown eyes, puddles of fudge, moist and glittered, Brenda could see why the girls loved him, penis fool that he was, Lord, delete that, delete it please and thank you but he does swing that penis around like it's tossing candy coins over a parade of sluts, sorry forgive me delete delete delete. Brenda secured the ladder up against the house, debated, but in the end kept her heels on, she was good on her toes like that. Her kid stood with her purse and his feet in the earth, squinting, the bottom of his tank rolled up a little and the hair on his stomach exposed, Feel a breeze? Brenda asked him, but he didn't get it. Brenda began her climb. Good thing you ain't wearing a skirt, her kid called up to her, else I'd be seeing something I don't want to see. He snorted, Yes ma'am, I'd be awash in barf if that was the case. Brenda prayed to sweet, delicious Jesus. Grace. Strength. Whatever else. During her pregnancy all those years ago she had anticipated a bond so strong that she would die for it. That had been true. But also true was how often she considered harming her child, just a little. Taser gun. Mace. Roundhouse kick. Judo chop. Good old windmill. Tires crunching over toes. She had never done any of it, she had once lobbed a small decorative pumpkin at his head, but that was the extent. Thank you Lord of Light, thank you chariot God. The gutter was caked, Brenda would need a tool of some sort. Trowel? she called down. Spade? Her kid emitted a low, indignant Uhhhhhhhhhh that Brenda interrupted with Spatula? Her kid trudged into the house, pausing to drop her purse into the dirt. The sky was pale blue now, all the gray diluted and drained, Brenda looked for the sun but didn't find it. The boy came out of the house with a small metal spatula Brenda recognized as her cookie spatula. Jesus was a child, Christ in a canoe, nature, nature, nature. Sweetest, Brenda said, ain't that the spatula I asked you about a few weeks ago? Oh yeah, the boy said, here it is, I guess, catch. Brenda watched the spatula blading through the air. Glinty arc. She caught it and her boy said, You need me out here the whole time? He bent to pick at a toe. I got shit on pause is the thing. But yell if you need anything. Brenda said, I got it, precious treasure, microwaved honeybun, go on inside. Brenda hacked at the gutter muck, Jésus Cristo preaching to the putas, but it would require more time than she had. She left the spatula staked in the muck. Maybe it'd attract lightning, she almost let herself complete the thought. She took off the 7-Eleven bag, went in to wash her hands, the front room of her kid's house featured her old sofa and a plate of nachos furred with mold. She went through to the kitchen, her kid in the TV room playing a video game, eyes glazed, the embroidered pillow Brenda brought over earlier in the month on the floor, a shoeprint across the face of the sunflower, and why she had thought her boy would want a sunflower pillow in his home she couldn't recall, her kid was right, it was faggoty, if faggoty meant nice, decorative, thoughtful. He had never forgiven her for the pumpkin incident. Lord God grant me a shovel! Brenda focused on her handwashing, the cucumber hand soap she'd brought over months before still full, the lather gray, then less gray, then a perfect bubbly white, this was the kind of satisfaction her kid would never know, never care to know. Perfect, bubbly, white. So simple! What are your plans for today? Brenda asked her kid. His foot rested on his knee, his foot as black with dirt as if it had been drawn there with charcoal. I don't know, was the answer. Well, jobs don't get themselves, Brenda said, forcing brightness into her voice. Good one, her boy said. On the television a black man with two swords cut the head off a woman in a metal bikini, the head screamed and the eyes rolled, the black man laughed and brandished his swords. Brenda's kid said, See what you did? Now I have to start all over. Holy Ghost on a tricycle, floating like a fart, Brenda didn't see what she did. Her kid was playing the woman in the bikini? Okay well, Brenda said. There was no reply, her kid was back in the game. The woman in the two-piece whipped her hair and did an elaborate scissoring flip. Brenda realized there was a good chance her kid had a boner. Okay well, Brenda said again. She'd always wanted to be a mother, she knew she'd be good at it, she wanted a close relationship with her son, when she pictured her own parents they were always staring just to the right of her, she didn't want that for her son, she wanted him to feel seen, loved, free to be himself, but now standing in his kitchen, counters covered in dried chili and cereal bowls and pizza boxes, trying not to see the tent he was pitching in his gym shorts, Brenda wondered if her parents were right to distance themselves, and she felt an unfamiliar warmth spread through her thinking of them, Mom, she thought, and Dad, Mom, Dad, Mom Dad, they were right, Mom with her tight-set hair and Dad with his bad toe pushing out of his slipper, they were right to just live their lives and not get involved. Brenda would leave now. Her kid would have to just figure it out, figure out how to clean his gutter clean his kitchen get a job contain his desire live in the world. She could see her purse out the window lumped in the dirt, and beyond was her car, she'd just had it washed, how it shone, she had to get to work, there was still that stretch of highway she had to drive, this was her life! Her own. And then she saw into her kid's bedroom. Saw the tangled hair tanned calf and single dollop breast staring dumbly out. The girl saying, Oh hey, in a pebbled voice, and there was the other breast now, two stunned eyes. The television shrieked, something was stabbed. Brenda's kid said, Don't look in there! but made no move to get up. Brenda continued on to the front door, closed the door behind her. The sky was a candy blue now. She bent for her purse, she bent into her car. The girl was beautiful. God in the grocery, this made her sad, she didn't know why. Did her kid appreciate it? Maybe that was it. Maybe it wasn't. But anyway, the highway.

ME AND HARDY

0

We took a wrong turn after Hardy dinged that kid on his bike. I was screaming and Hardy was probably working out in his head why he didn't stop and get that kid up off the ground, maybe cause the kid was all MY DAD'S GONNA JOHN DEERE YOUR PRIVATES WHEN I TELL HIM WHAT YOU DONE, and what that meant I still don't know, there was blood on the kid's mouth that was fake-looking, like he'd stopped for a Mountain Dew Code Red on his way to getting fucked up by our '96 Sentra, and Hardy twisting an eyebrow tween his thumb and forefinger like he do when he's stressed, and then Hardy put on the blinker, signaling to who I don't know, there was no one around, it was past 9:30 in the p.m. and dark as a denim quilt out, but it seemed to give Hardy purpose, that blinker, and we veered careful around the kid and made a right and Hardy kept to the speed limit and we drove calmly on like we was on our way to the market for apples and milk. The kid had pounded our car as we passed, and it made me feel better, I don't know about Hardy, but what kind of kid but a thug would pound on a car like that, no matter what the circumstances?

But anyway, that right turn took us off course, is the point. That's how we come to find ourselves driving through Acres Landing.

1

At the entrance to Acres Landing we saw a baby in a wagon next to a sign that said WAGON $2, BABY $5, OR 2 FOR $6. We drove on past that. Sometimes in life you have to just tell yourself something is a prank being played on someone else, and you can't worry about every baby in a wagon, I'm sure you get me.

Then we came to a Gas-n-Go that was the only source of light in a long while, and we stopped there so Hardy could fill er up and I could squeegee the fingerprints and blood off the car from the thug kid, and then I went in to use the ladies' and stared at my face cause I didn't have to pee but I didn't want to come out just yet, then when I did come out there was Hardy grappling with a fat woman in a tank top, over what I couldn't tell, the fat woman had him with one arm and Hardy's face was like a blood-colored, disappointed pumpkin, and when I crept up close I could see the woman's eyebrows was glittering, pierced from end to end I guess, there was a diamondy crust lining her nostrils, her ears was all metal, she had a jeweled sunburst on each cheek, glinty rings hung from her lips, and all in all she was jangling like a street whore's purse at sunup. Hardy was mouthing something at me, and finally I got it, and I reached into the glove compartment and come up with his blade and I jammed it in the woman's bready shuddering armfat, and Hardy broke free and kicked her in the bosom and she lost her purchase, that finally toppled her, and we broke out from that Gas-n-Go like I don't know what.

2

(Before the drive Hardy and I had mixed the last of his daddy's dried mushroom pellets into our bottle of Lipton iced tea that was more Aftershock than tea usually. I'm just telling you not cause you need to know our business but cause I can tell you wondering why we didn't start freaking our shit. The thug and the baby and the fatty and all. When you on psychedelics and liquor and no sleep you do your best not to freak your shit. Is what I'm saying.)

We drove for a while, Hardy got his breath and color back and the night hurtled by us like a train. Then the gravel started hitting the windshield and curving around into the car and stinging our arms and we rolled up the windows. It got worse, it got to where Hardy made to turn on the wipers till he realized that was stupid. Then we seen this glinting in the distance, getting brighter, then brighter, then we was right upon it, a bonfire with a stretcher hoisted up above it, and something black and writhing on the stretcher, and a cur dog hunched next to it, shitting at the stretcher's base, watching our car pass by with the slow turn of its mangy head, and then I threw up into my purse, that'll happen with mushrooms, or maybe it was the smell, either way.

3

Hardy told me the story about Santa Claus coming down the chimney, to make me feel better, he did the voice even, the Ho ho ho and all that mess, I actually don't care for that story cause I hate fat old men, all of them without question, but Hardy likes to tell it. Then we came to the dunes, the trees breaking off on both sides and the dunes revealed there in the night like monuments, like the fancy graves you sometimes see on TV, and I rolled down my window. Hardy got on me for not listening and we started in and he yanked my hair and I clawed his cheek, cause I ain't no delicate sunflower juddering in your grandma's vase, and I left jagged tracks dotted with blood, and he swerved trying to gouge my eye and screamed like a woman on a roller coaster so I rolled up my window and daubed at the blood with my shirt hem, and he shut up.

4

We had finally driven into the habitable portion of Acres Landing, a bunch of trailer homes and double wides at diagonals to the road, a trotting dog and the yellow glow of a cat's eyes, a boy with a pail out front his house doing nothing, just holding his pail, and I could relate to that, believe me. Doing nothing is the cross we have to bear. I waved to the boy and under the sickly yellow of his porch light I watched him mouth Stupid bitch at me, real slow, and then he reached into his pail and pulled out a fistful of something goopy and flung it at the car. I said, Mud, Hardy, that shitty child just threw mud at us, and then they was everywhere, more shitty children, all with mud, all chanting, Stupid Bitch. Stupid Bitch. I cracked the window and screamed, The name's Nancy, you shithead children, and then I could smell it, it wasn't mud but the children's own soupy excrement, some of it was green and nearly neon and I wondered was it Kool-Aid that done it or some kind of illness, and was that a whole intact kidney bean sliding down the windshield, this is the way my mind works due to all the detectiving, I can't help it nor do I try to, and anyway Hardy pushed on the gas and we flew out of there.

5

By now our high had leveled to the point where the world was a disappointment. Hardy lit a cigarette and another after that was done and then another and we passed them back and forth until the car was filled with smoke. We weren't taking no chances having the windows down. Hardy said, If we ever make it there I don't want to hear it from you when I drop you off. I hate it when he tells me how to act, and I was miserable enough to put the cigarette out in the tender flesh of my inner arm, but instead I rolled down my window cause Fuck it, see?

6

Hardy had wipered the shit off the windshield before it could dry and in its wake was a crescent moon of smeared clarity. Even so it was that time of night when you understand that the light of day is just a trick, a illusion, dumb as you are believing in it as you go about your grocery getting and your errands and your cheerful petting of a strange dog. I knew if I hadn't left that blade stuck in that lady's arm I'd have held it to Hardy's throat right then, all my high gone and the Lipton bottle dry as a bone, but see after the part in my imagining when I held the knife to Hardy's throat I couldn't figure out what came next, it just seemed like it'd be a lot of work, whatever it was.

7

I had fallen asleep finally and when I awoke the sun was flashing like a coin in a white dish, so bright I had to close my eyes again, I watched the ghost of the coin dart around my eyelids for a while, it helped with the deciding and it stayed there when I yanked the wheel, even as we started going over there was the coin, the car turning in the air, my heart in my throat and then in my stomach, Hardy with that roller-coaster-bitch screaming again, and all the while I made sure to keep my eyes closed, cause I needed the dark, see, for the courage or whatever, and then we had come to a stop and I opened my eyes and we was upside down and the blood oozing out of Hardy's ears like red candle wax, slow and thick, I thought he was a goner but then I saw him breathe so I pushed my way out the window and climbed back up to the road and flagged you down and let you drive me, and all right fine, to answer your question I left him there cause he wasn't finished being there yet, I don't know what else to tell you.

BIRTHDAY LUNCHEON

Your brother's pregnant girlfriend got her leg up on the desserts cart, thrusting her hips over the lemon meringue, your daddy's favorite, you can see the words *Sweet Bitch* in glitter script in the front part of her undies every time the cart rolls a little, which it does a lot, she dancing so thoroughly her shoe fell off a song ago, she bent to get it but the bending didn't fit with the beat of the song so she let it be, and you felt like maybe that meant she was smarter than you gave her credit for, and you thought that even when she dipped her toe in a lava cake and then tried to lick it off till she realized she don't bend that far and did a sloppy, arcing kick so she could brandish that toe in your daddy's face, your daddy with that paper cone askew on his head, that elastic cutting into all that flesh at his jaw, your daddy with his small black eyes and his big wet mouth and that nipple of mashed potatoes on his shirt, your daddy who once asked you, could you come here, come closer, and belched your name right into your face and asked you to guess what he ate for dinner, your daddy who told your brother ladies'd get wet over a cocktail wiener if it was wrapped in twenties, your daddy who told you if you went to the Walmart past ten at night you'd be raped by a gang of blacks in the lightbulbs aisle, and later it changed to a gang of Mexicans, your daddy who punched your brother in the mouth the night he told about getting his girlfriend pregnant, your daddy who called that girlfriend a slut Oreo on Christmas Day, your daddy who could surely read the words on your brother's girlfriend's panties crotch despite his cataracts, your daddy who swatted that foot out his face like a poisonous insect, your daddy raised up that fist, that hammered clump of knuckles, and pounded the table so hard his little sippy cup of tea and gin fell off the table, your brother saying, Well, Pop, and your daddy saying his meanest, something beyond words, something close to Nnnnnnnnnnnnnn, gums wet and pink as something just birthed, and you just watching that tea and gin spurt out your daddy's straw and onto the crazy quilt of a carpet they had in this place, and when you looked up the old man from the next table was behind your brother's girlfriend, slapping her thigh and bouncing on his toes like he was playing at riding a horse, and your brother's girlfriend moving slower cause it was a slow song now, both her feet on the ground, eyes closed, and the old man not getting it, riding his horse out of time with the beat, it was unsettling, it was rude, you found yourself muttering, Are you serious? Are you serious? like you was tasered or something, your step-aunt leaning across the table and salad-mouthing, Serious bout what, hon? and your brother twitching like he'd just come to life, your brother saying, Serious bout your face mole, and your step-aunt dabbing at her face with the corner of a napkin, that mole the color of Thousand Island dressing, ringed in red now from being dabbed at, your daddy's dead wife's sister who your daddy had to stay the night every now and again, they was a pair, your daddy in his wheelchair and your step-aunt in her scooter, your brother told you they just rammed wheels and tallied that up as sex, the jostling was enough he said, and now when you get the chance to have some yourself you think of it as jostling, Jostle me, you want to say into a man's neck, Jostle me good, your brother's girlfriend walking the old man back to his seat now, limping on her one shoe, the old man's family eyeing your brother's girlfriend with red faces and slit eyes, the old man's daughter saying, All right now, your brother's girlfriend saying, You welcome, sug, stopping on her way back to the table to pick her undies out her ass, your brother arranging the cutlery around her plate like it was the return of the mother of Jesus, your daddy eating his meat loaf like a slice of pizza, your daddy didn't take no puree, I eat sholidsh, your brother mixing your daddy another sippy, your brother's girlfriend cutting up that dish of meringue into little pellets for your daddy to maw on, your step-aunt fluffing her bangs with one hand and worrying that mole with the other, your daddy's legs poking out his shorts like something veined and obscene, your daddy who you told when you thought they was goblins in your closet, your daddy who said, Got that right and snapped off the light, and now you thinking how you ain't hungry for dessert, you thinking how you don't know what you hungry for, you eyeing that carpet and thinking how there was a time when a spill like that'd remind you quick just how much a man your daddy was, all teeth eyes belt and fist.

LETA'S MUMMY

Leta got a mummy up under the floorboards. You could see it rising when her daddy's got the TV too loud or when her brother lights up the toilet with his beer shits. That mummy is a shit-hating kind of mummy. One thing about Leta's mummy is, it'll take a bite if you ain't paying mind. So you got to always try to look like you don't taste all that good. Leta lost a chunk of her hand to that mummy and the worst thing is, it just gummed on it for a while and let it thud to the floor along with the rest of its cheek. Then it bayed like its heart was broken and shrunk down into the floor. Leta's daddy told her hush, least he didn't get you in the titty or the face, and I nodded and Leta tried to nod, but it's hard to when your mouth can't close cause you screaming.

I spend a lot of time over to Leta's cause my momma works nights and when she don't she is on our back porch with her Dixie cup. Sometimes she get to wailing and I just got to go. Then I come back in the morning and wash out her cup like nothing. To me the worst part about the mummy ain't its appetite for flesh or the fact that it smell like infinity diapers, all on fire. It's when it bays like it do, cause it sounds like my momma. Both of em just crying like they stuck, like they brain got sucked out and tears put back in its place.

Sometimes it feels good to shake a fist and yell, That fuckin mummy! right along with Leta's daddy. Only when I do it I am thinking of my momma.

At school ever since her hand got chewed up Leta is the shit. Girls be chewing they hands all through class to get em nice and mangled, and boys be offering up the high five and then saying, No, the other one, when Leta raises her good hand. In science class Mr. Howe puts pictures of dead people on the projector, some of em all wrapped up like Leta's mummy, and explains how when a mummy is a mummy they ain't rising up to stink up your living room. Leta got her head down, but I can tell her eyes are open, she is hearing every word. I guess I see his point, it seems like a horror that can't be real, but I raise my hand and tell Mr. Howe he's a dumbass anyway.

My momma comes to school to hear what a bitch I am. Her hair all ruined to one side and dried-up spit at the corner of her mouth, coat on over her nightdress. Might as well be wrapped up and tossed under the house. In front of the principal she puts her hand on my arm and says, You got to try harder. When he ain't looking that hand goes hard, mummified, digs in. It burns and I can't help it, I get tears. I put my hand over hers and dig in just as hard. When the principal looks up he says, Ain't that nice, and we let go.

That mummy never bit at me, but when it do I am prepared to bite back.

In detention the retarded boy asks me could I give the mummy a letter he wrote. I feel too tired to tell the boy that the mummy ain't got eyes, or a brain, has never bayed about a hankering to take up reading. I just take the letter and put my head back down. Later I see that the letter is a drawing of the retarded boy and the mummy holding hands out front of the library. When the mummy rises up to windmill at Leta's brother that night, I flick the letter at it and it comes back all gummed to a pulp, a brown turdy glob me and Leta got to clean away soon as the mummy is done with its terror.

Leta's family starts going to church to see if God can do something about the mummy. Leta says she's fixing to pray for the mummy to be a people again, so she can put its hand in her momma's old blender, see how it likes that. I ain't going to church with them cause I seen how the women fall to tears and the men raise up they hands and the pastor just yelling at all of them till his face is black how the world is ending and it's like yeah, well, the world ended for that mummy and it seems just fuckin dandy with it.

One Sunday my momma starts in with her cup, from the kitchen telling me I had a daddy but he was burnt to a crisp over to the war, and this would move me but for the fact that Momma told me a while back my daddy was in jail, and before that my daddy was the mayor and I shouldn't tell no one. Oh, my momma says, oh oh oh. Crying over her cup for whatever daddy she pleases. Bye, I told her.

Leta's house was empty cause they was at church, but I could hear the mummy inside, they'd left the TV on cause Leta's daddy thinks it'd help tire the mummy out while they gone.

It ain't like the mummy can see you, cause where its eyes was is just hollows with glints of slime, but that mummy lurched my way soon as I came into that living room. Ennh, it said at me. Yeah? I said at it. It windmilled, flinging its tatters my way, feet stuck planted dumb in the floorboards like always. Ennnnnnh!

That fuckin mummy. How it ate Leta's brother's girlfriend's braid one time, and she ain't never come back. How her daddy had to learn the Internet just to find out how to get rid of a mummy, and then there wasn't even no useful information, and now every time we got to go on there for school we got to close a dozen of them pop-up things. Leta so shameful about her stump hand. How living here would be way better than living with Momma but for this fuckin mummy.

Ennh, the mummy said again. Mad as usual, mad at nothing and everything, take your pick. Like how Momma could choose when to be sad, when to get all brainless. Well, I can make choices too, I screamed at that mummy.

I went into the kitchen and set a pot to boil. When the water burbled up I brought it over, close as I cared to get, and tossed it over the mummy's raggedy head. Threw Leta's daddy's coffee mug at its crotch. Flung Leta's brother's metal bat at it. Threw a lamp, threw the basket of dusty magazines Leta's momma left behind. Tried to throw the TV, but there were too many cords to untangle. Threw all the VHSs in the drawer, then threw the drawer. Threw pillows a fruit bowl the remote the TV guide a cinnamon candle the curtain rod a dining chair another dining chair Leta's daddy's best knife a frozen chicken another dining chair Leta's math book three old Big

Gulps a hamster cage and a broom at it and when I got tired I squirted lighter fluid at it and lit that fuckin mummy on fire. He didn't even yell.

When Leta and her family came home and saw the pile of ashes, saw all I had done to kill the mummy, it was clear I wasn't welcome there no more.

I went home and poured Momma's bottles down the drain, one by one. She carried on about it, but only for a little while. She stayed quiet after that, out on her porch, holding her empty cup, night after night. Like she was mostly dead. And I guess I could see why Leta's family got so ticked at me. Wishing something dead was a whole lot different from actually seeing it dead. I tried to regret it, I still try.

DARREN'S BABY GIRL

Darren says I'm his baby girl. He says that cause I tell him every day, I'm your baby girl. I'm your baby girl ain't I?

You're my baby girl. We're in the bed, me under the covers and him on top of the covers cause it's a hotel and he thinks the sheets are blessed with the skin cells and gushings of a million other people, people we don't know, gross people. I don't tell him in my experience the blanket's where the real action is at, pushing through the door tequila mouth on tequila mouth slam buttons popping off clothes bunched to the floor and *ploom* you land on the bed and no one takes the time to pull back the coverlet. At least the sheets get bleached. But I don't tell him that cause I'm his baby girl and so how would I know? I wouldn't.

If Darren was into it I'd wear a diaper and suck on my ba-ba, but he seems to want a baby girl that can talk, do her numbers, say her pleases and thank yous. If Darren was into it I'd call him Daddy, what do I care, I never called anyone Daddy in my whole life, but Darren ain't my daddy, he has made that clear. I tried Uncle Darren once, but that didn't go over neither.

Now I just try not to say his name.

Darren's got the TV on, going from channel to channel, enamel-haired newspeople staring at us, not blinking, back to weather, over to weather, Ken, how's the weather? Nobody's got anything to say, Darren says. Not one real thing.

That's a relief, I answer, and I feel guilty cause would a baby girl use the word relief? To distract him I get out of bed, walk slowly in front of the TV on my way to the bathroom so he can see the pink ruffles of my nightie, the pink scoops of my bare ass.

Sometimes Darren likes to listen to me go, but tonight don't seem like one of those nights, he barely glanced at my nakedness when I walked past, and that is another relief, cause I don't actually have to pee.

The bathroom is the color of jaundice, soaps in paper, a single vinyl shower curtain, towels bleached so many times the white had curdled, chipped toilet seat. In the trash can, a magazine insert advertising a discounted subscription to *Bass Fishing International* if you subscribe to *Bass Fishing USA*, the petals of a tissue dotted with blood. The tissue is Darren's, the insert must be from the guest before us. I wish he'd left the whole magazine. Darren don't let me read much, so I got to take it wherever I can get it.

I flush to keep up the ruse, walk slowly in front of the TV again. Now it's the blips and roar of a game show. My body's all warm, I know without looking Darren is watching me.

You forget something? Darren asks.

Um, I say. I twirl a finger in my hair. I feel lit up, like a glittering flashing game show sign.

You forgot your bottoms, baby girl, he says, but he is pleased, it's clear.

Oh no, I say. I pretend to try to cover up without really covering anything up. Want me to put them on?

Too late, Darren says. Now you got to be punished.

I know what he means. I got to get to his belt before he can, so I let out a giggle, run at him. I work his belt off, push it under my pillow when he's got his shirt over his head. Darren's a quick man, so I don't have to roll around on that coverlet for long, and he's fast with the spanking this time, just a few claps before he flattens to sleep.

I used to watch Darren sleep, watch his every rising breath, but after a while that can get old, even what with his twitching feet and his shriveled penis, looking for all the world like a sea creature ripped from its shell.

I put the TV back on the news. A woman in a blue suit, backlit by flames. Strands of her blond hair whipping in the hot wind. The pink jewel of her mouth moving slowly, taking its time with the words. Nothing can stop Darren from sleeping. Hold a gun to his head, set his bed on fire, it don't matter, Darren will sleep right through it.

I get up carefully, put on my jeans. The hall outside our room smells like the carpet, cigarettes and feet and chlorine from the pool they got on the third floor, which is where I'm going since I know there's a soda machine. Darren don't let me have soda, I got to sneak it.

A lady in a scooter is parked at the edge of the pool, watching her boy tread water with one arm and eat a naked hot dog with the other. A streamer of smoke from her hand. Funny how cigarette smoke smells so different from the smoke from a real fire. I could say what this lady had for dinner if I cared to stand in her blow space. A real fire ain't so personal. They should call that kind of smoke something different.

I know he ain't supposed to eat in the pool, the lady says. He knows it too, that's how come he's so careful.

He could eat a whole pizza in there for all I care, I tell her.

Whoever heard of a indoor pool? the boy asks. A wet nugget of hot dog tumbles down his chin and into the pool.

For all you care? his momma repeats. She drops her cigarette, backs over it with her scooter. She had a wayward eye, dull as an old button.

I just came for a soda, I say. I ain't here to swim.

They don't refill the machine until next week, the woman says. Drink the pool water, for all I care.

You hear about that Circle K burning down? I ask her. I just saw it on the news.

I used to work there, she says. Before my accident. So?

I didn't say that I figured her accident was probably eating the shelves clean of all the Krispy Kremes. Her boy watching me with the eyes of an animal weighing its options but leaning toward napping, one eye nearly turned, give it another year and he'd have that dull button eye just like his momma.

Well, I say. That fire wasn't no accident. Someone lit a match and put it on the shelf with the tampons. Just like if you was to be rolled into that pool to get yourself a drink of the pool water wouldn't be no accident.

Her boy's wet mouth opens wide, someone get the hook. What'd that lady just say? he asks.

For a second I almost say, What lady? Hard not to see myself as a true baby girl, someone close to this fish boy's age, someone he might try his chances with.

I know you, the lady says.

No, I tell her, you don't.

I do, she says, like she's just won at cards. She tips her head, it's the flat button eye's turn to see, it rolls into place and this is a shock. I know you, girl, she says.

I know you, baby girl. Darren with that big hand around that shovel, the caramel-brown of his forearms, all muscle and vein. All throbbing tender life. And my manager saying, After this customer go on and take your break. Yeah, Darren said. Take your break. Come with me. I never saw him before in my life. Maybe he'd never seen me but he sure acted like he had. Me at the cashier station and my momma working in the jewelry section, we'd go home and eat leftovers and watch the *Late Show*. Or. Come with me. I did, and I found out why the shovel, and I been his baby girl ever since. Easy to let someone think they know you, long as you become who they think you are.

I got you, the lady says. I got you good. She reaches down between her legs, brings out a cell phone. You better run, she says.

I know she's right. I should run. But I don't. I walk slowly out. The hallway smell again, my smeared reflection in the elevator doors. The doors open, a woman in pink curlers gets off, I get on. I can't decide what button to push. I think how I should have kicked the phone out the lady's hands. I think how Darren only used that shovel the one time. I think how I left my smock in the break room, how that game show glittered from the TV, how it ain't so easy to see the glitter sometimes. I think how my momma probably took that smock home to wash it. I think how I lit the match, how at first it was just a tiny flame, a dot of glitter. I think how I'll wake Darren up, get him his pants, tell him we got to go. Put my hair in braids while he dresses. Wait for him to ask me who I am.

DON'T KISS ME

I WANT TO TELL THE WOMAN ACROSS FROM ME THAT IF YOU SPRITZ AIR FRESHENER INTO YOUR PURSE IT WILL NO LONGER SMELL SO PURSE-LIKE

BUT SEE THEN I WOULD HAVE TO EXPLAIN HOW I AM AFRAID OF THE SMELL OF NEW ITEMS, AND JUST THIS MORNING I CONFESSED HOW I AM AFRAID IT IS SALIVA COMING OUT OF THE SHOWER SPIGOT SO I DON'T WANT TO PUSH IT TOO FAR WITH HER

SHE IS BLOND

LIKE IF YOU BUY YOUR CHILD A NEW PAIR OF MARY JANES THE LEATHER STRAP SMELLS LIKE A LEATHER STRAP AND I CANNOT ABIDE IT

THIS WOMAN ACROSS FROM ME HAS A VOICE LIKE WHAT I IMAGINE BUTTERSCOTCH WOULD SOUND LIKE WERE IT NOT THE HARDENED DIARRHEAL TURD I AM CONVINCED IT TO BE

HER FACE IS LIKE WHAT A BABY'S FACE WOULD LOOK LIKE SHOULD IT SUDDENLY BECOME ATTACHED TO AN ADULT HEAD

MY HUSBAND DRANK FOUR TEQUILA SUNRISES AT THE HOLIDAY PARTY AND INFORMED ME SHE WAS ATTRACTIVE

LATER HE VOMITED DOWN HIS TIE

I THREW THAT TIE AWAY BECAUSE THAT WAS THE MONTH MY WASHER AND DRYER BECAME INHABITED BY GHOSTS OF BLACK MEN ASKING TO FONDLE MY GOURDS

IT IS NOT POSSIBLE TO BABY-FY YOUR FACE, I HAVE LOOKED IT UP

SOMETIMES I THINK ABOUT TAPING A PHOTO OF THIS WOMAN OVER MY FACE DURING ALONE TIME WITH MY HUSBAND, YOU HAVE TO BE CREATIVE IN A MARRIAGE SOMETIMES

BUT THE ONLY PHOTO I HAVE OF HER IS FROM HER CHRISTMAS CARD, SHE IS HOLDING HER CHILD AND WEARING ANTLERS AND I AM AFRAID THAT IS TOO MUCH STIMULANT FOR MY HUSBAND

THIS WOMAN EATS LIVE CUCUMBER, I HAVE SEEN IT WITH MY OWN EYES

ON OCCASION I HAVE CONVINCED THIS WOMAN TO VENTURE OUT AND EAT LUNCH WITH ME

I LIKE THE OLIVE GARDEN BUT THIS WOMAN PREFERS OUTBACK

IF WE DRIVE SEPARATE SOMETIMES I DROP BY THE OLIVE GARDEN ANYWAY

IT DISGUSTS ME TO SEE A GROWN WOMAN EAT A SALAD BUT I AM DEDICATED, I FORGIVE THIS WOMAN EACH TIME THOUGH I KNOW THE

FLECKS OF LETTUCE ARE SLOWLY DISINTEGRATING HER ESOPHAGUS

YOU CAN'T SAVE EVERYONE

I HAVE A BLOND WIG, IT CAME PACKAGED WITH THE MERMAID COSTUME I BOUGHT FOR MY CHILD AT THE CVS THE YEAR SHE WAS IN HIDING, THE WIG DOES NOT FIT MY HEAD AND THAT IS WHAT THE GLUE IS FOR

I WEAR THAT WIG SOMETIMES WHEN I'M ALONE AND I MAKE MYSELF A SALAD OF PRETZELS DRIZZLED WITH TABASCO

I FEEL CLOSEST TO THE BLOND WOMAN IN THESE MOMENTS

SOMETIMES I CALL THE WOMAN ON THE PHONE EVEN THOUGH SHE IS RIGHT ACROSS FROM ME

I SAY, I SEE YOU

IF YOU WAIT FOR THIS WOMAN TO VISIT THE LADIES' YOU CAN SIT IN HER CHAIR, IT DOES NOT KNOW WHO IS SITTING IN IT DESPITE WHAT YOU MAY BELIEVE

I ONCE ATE THIS WOMAN'S PEN CAP FROM THE WARM WOMB OF COMFORT I KNOW HER CHAIR TO BE

I WAS CHEWING IT AS I HAD SEEN HER DO BUT THEN I LOST CONTROL

I WAS NOT POPULAR IN HIGH SCHOOL

I WATCHED PROM FROM THE SAFETY OF THE FRONT SEAT OF MY FATHER'S CAR, I USED BINOCULARS

AFTER, I WENT TO THE DENNY'S AND WATCHED THEM ALL FROM A BOOTH AT THE BACK

I USED BINOCULARS

I MET MY HUSBAND ON THE INTERNET, HE WAS THE ONLY OTHER PERSON AFRAID OF WIND ASIDE FROM ME THAT I COULD FIND

DURING OUR FIRST LUNCH THIS WOMAN HELD ME WHILE I CRIED, WIND HAD TOUCHED MY FACE ON THE WALK TO THE CAR AND I KNEW THAT MEANT A CARTOON DEMON HAD MOLESTED ME

FOR CHRISTMAS THIS WOMAN GAVE ME A SATCHEL OF POTPOURRI, THERE WAS NO CARD AND I WAS EMBARRASSED FOR HER

REGARDLESS I ATE IT ALL ON THE DRIVE HOME

I GAVE HER A COUPON FOR A FRIENDSHIP SNUGGLE, IT WAS EASY, I PRINTED IT OFF THE INTERNET

I ALSO E-MAILED IT TO HER

SHE HAS NOT CASHED IT IN BUT EVERY DAY IS A NEW DAY

I GUESS I LOVE THIS WOMAN

IT GNAWS AT ME

BUT SEE IT'S GOT TO WHERE THESE DAYS I CAN'T TELL WHAT'S WORTH CONFESSING ANYMORE

ACKNOWLEDGMENTS

An assault of kisses are owed to featherproof books, and Zach Dodson in particular. To Jac Jemc, for her early enthusiasm for the collection. To Mary Hamilton, who brought out the short-story writer in me. Amelia Gray, for terrifying and inspiring. Emily Bell, who is a badass. Jim Rutman, for helping champion my work. Matt Trupia and Sarah Grainer, writers and cherished friends who made me weirder. And finally, to my husband, without whom I shudder to think.